IN DEEP

BY MICHAEL SEGEDY

Copyright © 2012 by Michael Segedy
ISBN: 9798759001355

All rights reserved. Except as permitted under the US Copyright Act of 1976, no part of this publication may be reproduced, distributed or transmitted in any form or by any means, or stored in a database or retrieval system, without the prior permission of the author.

This novel is dedicated to my loving wife, Ursula, and to our beautiful daughter, Paloma. Without their help, and their belief in me and my work, this novel would never have happened.

"The only thing necessary for the triumph of evil is for good men to do nothing." — Edmund Burke

1

The lift off in the twin engine Cessna 340 was smooth and uneventful. It was a bright, cloudless day over Lima, Peru and the weather report that Senator David Kursten received from the American Embassy promised a pleasant flight. As chairman of the Senate Judiciary Committee on Crime, Drug Trafficking, and Terrorism, the senator's official purpose in Peru was to determine to what extent the Peruvian government had implemented measures to reduce coca production.

Colonel Luis Antonio Vargas sat across the aisle from the senator, lecturing him on the Peruvian government's vigorous anti-drug campaign. He boasted that in the last month Peru had destroyed over a hundred hectares of coca. In a sting operation, the national police had stopped a shipment of four hundred kilos of cocaine to the US. This had been big news worldwide, and staunch, anti-drug senators on the committee back home had used the cocaine bust to illustrate the success of the War on Drugs abroad.

The senator, a tall man with a full head of gray hair and a large Teddy bear-like physique, listened politely, but he needed more than the colonel's words to convince him of the Peruvian government's efforts. He wanted to see the eradicated coca fields. The colonel had to demonstrate that the Peruvians were seriously complying. If not, then the senator was determined to do everything he could to defeat the bill in Congress authorizing additional aid to Peru to fight the drug war. Kursten suspected the CIA was using DEA money to combat the left wing insurgency in this poverty stricken nation, and that the drug eradication program was just a front. He had even dared to bring this up during one of the congressional hearings.

"What you see below, Senator," the colonel said, pointing to a large defoliated swath of jungle, "is one of the farms we decommissioned last week." The colonel, a round faced, middle-aged man with thick glasses, opened his leather case, took out a pair of binoculars, and passed them to the congressman.

Senator Kursten adjusted the focus as he looked out the small oval window at a portion of defoliated jungle 5000 feet below. He was about to call out to co-pilot Major Spanchek, a US Army horticulturist, and ask him to take a look at the area of defoliation, but decided to wait and hear the colonel out. Major Spanchek had accompanied the senator for the purpose of identifying coca fields and providing him with technical advice pertaining to the cultivation of coca.

"As you can see, Senator, this hacienda is large. It has around ten hectares of land dedicated solely to cultivating coca. Had that is. The campesinos have agreed to plant coffee beans and soybeans. Also, bananas." A smirk formed on the portly colonel's face as he boasted of the government's accomplishments.

Before Congressman Kursten could respond, the curtain between the cabin and the cockpit slid open and a tall man in a major's uniform stepped into the narrow passageway wielding a Browning 9 mm semi-automatic. With a slight grin on his clean-shaven face, he stood over the two middle-aged gentlemen as they looked up at him in total shock and disbelief.

The colonel blurted out, *"Que te pasa!"* while the gray-haired congressman sat frozen in his seat, speechless, not knowing if what he was witnessing was for real or was some bizarre joke.

"You'll have to excuse me, gentlemen, for the interruption," said the tall figure dressed in a freshly starched uniform. "I hope you don't take any of this too personally. It's just business. Nothing more."

Smiling ironically, he pulled the trigger. A bullet exploded from the gun and struck the colonel in the chest right above his heart, thrusting him back in his seat.

The tall figure watched as the colonel's body seemed to stiffen and then relax as his head fell back against the head rest and his vacant eyes stared up at the ceiling. His mouth hung agape, as though he were about to ask a question but was caught in mid-sentence.

In absolute panic, the senator let go of the documents resting in his lap as his hands shot up in front of him in a futile and somewhat comical attempt to protect himself.

The major fired another shot. This one went through the congressman's outstretched hand and struck him between his eyes. His head bucked backward for a split second before falling forward against his chest. As his large body tilted to the side and was about to tumble into the aisle, the major raised his leg and gave it a solid kick that sent it back in the seat.

Then, as if out of respect for the senator, he leaned over the colonel's body, grabbed the crumpled senator by his lapels and lifted him upright in his seat. He removed the handkerchief from the senator's suit pocket and wiped away the tiny stream of blood trickling down the senator's forehead where the bullet had entered. When he finished, he neatly folded the bloody handkerchief and placed it back in the dead man's pocket. Cocking his head to the side, he admired his work, smiling wryly while he mused over the frozen features on the senator's face, his pale blue eyes staring up at him blankly and his mouth parted slightly as though in a speechless prayer.

Turning on his heel, the major took a bold step forward and then strolled into the cockpit. Slumped over on his side in the pilot's seat was a young Peruvian captain, the front of his shirt soaked through in blood, the bright red liquid still oozing from the gaping slit in his throat. The major snatched a parachute from behind the seat and quickly strapped it on. He reached across the body to the control panel, clicked a switch and killed the left engine. Instantly the plane began to tilt to the side. He adjusted a wing flap to straighten the plane and then pushed in slightly on the control wheel to put the plane in a gradual descent.

Seconds later he returned to the cabin, pulled down sharply on the cabin door latch, and shoved the door open. A torrent of air rushed in ruffling his clothes and sending the blood soaked documents, which lay at the feet of the senator, flying to the back of the cabin.

Steadying himself against the blast of air ripping through the open hatch, he turned to his two dead passengers. "*Adios, amigos.*" Then gripping the sides of the opening, he pulled himself forward and jumped into the blue space below.

2

Ambassador Wenton stood behind his large mahogany desk paging through a pile of documents he'd received from the DEA. He was a tall man in his early sixties, over six feet two and still trim and fit. He'd been the US Ambassador to Peru for nearly three years and had also served as ambassador to Nicaragua, several years after the Contra affair had ended and the country was on its long, arduous journey toward recovery. Today promised to be one hell of a day. He'd just gotten off the phone with Peru's minister of the interior and earlier in the morning with the assistant secretary of state in Washington, D.C. In the next few minutes, he expected to be briefed by Bill Henkly, the DEA chief.

He wasn't looking forward to meeting with Henkly. He didn't like him much, or spooks like Singler, Henkly's buddy. In the ambassador's opinion, Henkly dedicated himself more to serving his ego than his country. Though the same couldn't be said of Singler, he thought that he liked him even less. Singler's cheerless, bureaucratic demeanor completely turned him off. At least Henkly occasionally smiled. Apart from Carl Singler's cheerlessness, he was an aloof prick with a cold, hard exterior that set him on edge. Maybe it came with being a spook. He'd probably worked hard on projecting his hard-ass demeanor. During his years in the diplomatic corps, the ambassador had known his fair share. Guys like him saw themselves as cool, tough guardians of democracy, fighting the evil empires that threatened America's existence. We needed guardians, Wenton reflected, since America had to protect itself from ruthless governments and deranged terrorists. But our intelligence services could use more refined agents, maybe with a touch of James Bond. Operatives infused with much more humanity than Singler ever evinced. For sure, Singler was no James Bond. He was about as suave and charming as Arnold Schwarzenegger in *The Terminator*.

When it came to negotiating, Henkly and Singler viewed anyone opposing America's interests as dog shit on the bottom of their new Reeboks. Although Wenton loved his country dearly, he had trouble seeing everything as black or white. As we versus them. He'd begun his career as an academic, not as a civil servant or political figure. For years he'd taught Latin American history at the University of Virginia. Shortly after winning the election, President Clinton appointed him as Ambassador to Nicaragua. He spent three years there before becoming ambassador to Panama, where he'd served for seven years before accepting the ambassadorship in Peru. After more than a decade serving in the diplomatic corps, he still had a hard time getting close to his staff, the State Department career folks, especially those who had served in the military. He sometimes thought that they suspected his patriotism wasn't staunch enough. Recently, he'd begun to wonder why he'd given up his academic career at the University of Virginia to become a diplomat. Or why he'd remained one for so long when his true love was scholarship, not politics and business.

Ambassador Wenton's reverie was broken suddenly when Henkly stepped into his office. He greeted the ambassador and then sat down in a black leather chair directly in front of the ambassador's desk.

"Well, Mr. Henkly, what's the latest?" Wenton asked, peering over his glasses.

"Yesterday a small group of Shining Path insurgents were reported eighty kilometers northeast of Tingo María," Henkly began, sitting cross-legged, tapping his pen against the yellow legal pad resting in his lap. "That's relatively close to where the plane carrying Congressman Kursten and Major Spanchek went down, Mr. Ambassador."

"It's too early to determine what happened," Wenton said, guessing where Henkly was going. "Nonetheless, Washington wants some answers. And soon. I was on the phone with the assistant Secretary of State a few minutes ago. He'd like an update as soon as we have something solid. What do we have on the crash specifically, Mr. Henkly? I'm talking about hard facts that I can communicate to Washington."

"We have reason to believe that Rafael López's extradition to the US may be connected to the downing of the plane," Henkly offered.

Wenton knew better than to be baited by Henkly. "I'd prefer not to use the expression 'downing of the plane,'" Wenton rejoined, perturbed by Henkly's less than subtle attempt at manipulation. "This whole business could escalate into something larger than we wish it to. Right now there's no reason to make any direct connection between the crash and the terrorists."

"There'd been threats," Henkly continued stubbornly, unabashed, "and the proximity of the guerillas to the crash site is hardly coincidental, Mr. Ambassador. Our intelligence reports confirm that the Shining Path has acquired Javelin LML surface to air missiles. They are perfect for shooting down planes flying at low altitudes. According to our reports, earlier in the year a half a dozen Javelins disappeared from a Peruvian arsenal. Crooked security officials allegedly sold the missiles to the Shining Path."

"But firing on a plane with a US senator aboard? Why would the terrorists risk US military intervention? Doesn't seem likely. Now the drug lords, that's a possibility. Granted, the Shining Path has become involved today with the narco-traffickers, but not enough to warrant killing a US senator. They used to charge the narcos a fee for their services. But that was years ago, at the height of the Shining Path insurgency. Today we have a handful of *Senderistas* operating in the Huallaga Valley abetting the drug lords. You said that a small group was reported near by the crash. How small of a group? A half a dozen?"

"No exact numbers were given," Henkly replied glumly.

"Shooting down an American plane with a US congressman aboard and inviting a costly US military reprisal, simply to please the drug lords, is highly questionable," he continued, clearly agitated by Henkly's flimsy argument.

"But we know for certain that the terrorists are active in the area where the plane crashed," Henkly insisted, playing the only card he had.

"Proximity of a few guerrillas to the plane crash is not enough. You'll need more than that. The Upper Huallaga Valley is no longer swarming with terrorists. At least that's my reading of your sector's reports. For Christ's sake, this is not the 80s or 90s. The Shining Path movement has pretty much been crushed. A few terrorists near…"

Ambassador Wenton noticed the intercom flashing. Frustrated by Henkly's dogged persistence to build a case against the rebels, he tossed the documents he had been holding in his hand onto his desk, reached across and pressed the flashing red button.

"Mr. Ambassador, Mr. Brinton is here. Says it's urgent," announced the staticky voice from the intercom.

"Thank you. Please send him in."

John Brinton, the DCM, pushed the door open and stepped into the ambassador's office. As the Deputy Chief of Mission, he was the second in command at the American Embassy. He was also an old friend of Wenton's and had worked with him in Managua. He was a short, stodgy man, with a shiny pate, about the same age as Wenton, and also an ex-professor. He had a funny little mustache that was tweaked off bluntly on each side. Many of the American Embassy staff referred to the two of them as Laurel and Hardy. This particular morning there was nothing remotely funny in his demeanor. The expression on his pudgy face was grave, and the way he gritted his teeth gave the impression he had a bad case of indigestion or heart burn.

"Good morning, Mr. Ambassador," he said clearing his throat. He glanced at Henkly sitting stiffly in the chair in front of the ambassador's desk, nodded and said, "Good morning, Mr. Henkly."

"Is it, Mr. Brinton?" Wenton asked skeptically.

Rarely did Brinton's small, blue eyes display such emotion, and at the moment, the pained expression in them did not herald good news.

"Colonel Montero, the Peruvian colonel in charge in Tingo María, just called. He went out to the crash site earlier this morning." Brinton paused and looked again at Henkly.

"Yes?" Wenton asked.

"The colonel said they found fragments of a missile lodged in one of the panels of the fuselage."

"Shit! That's not what I wanted to hear. Anything else?"

"Yes, they found what was left of the bodies of the four who were on board." Brinton bit his lip and looked down before continuing. Then clearing his throat he went on. "Colonel Montero said he received a call from a Shining Path rebel claiming responsibility."

Wenton shot a glance at Henkly. Pasted across his face was this arrogant expression that said, "*I told you so!*" The ambassador felt like strangling the bastard.

"Were there any witnesses to the crash? Any *campesinos* that might have seen what happened?"

Although the colonel claiming that the Shining Path shot down the plane was more than enough proof for Henkly that the rebels were involved, Wenton did not necessarily trust Colonel Montero. After what he had read in the *Truth and Reconciliation Commission Report*, concluded back in 2003, he had reasons to doubt Peruvian military reports on rebel activity.

"I asked him the same question," Brinton replied. "He said no. There was no one within miles of the crash site when they arrived." Brinton's face looked as pale as the report he held in his hand.

"Well, if the Shining Path did shoot down the plane," Wenton sighed, "things are definitely going to heat up. This will be seen as an act of terror against the United States." With an unsteady hand, he reached slowly across his desk and pressed down the intercom button.

Henkly had already sprung up from his chair, eager and ready.

"*Yes, Mr. Ambassador?*" his secretary's voice answered.

He looked directly at Henkly standing in front of him with his arms crossed, as attentive as a pit bull waiting for a bone to be thrown his way.

"Tell him that at the assistant secretary's earliest convenience that I need to talk to him, that we have an important development on the plane crash. Thanks."

"*Yes, Mr. Ambassador. I'll get right on it.*"

"I'll see what news I can get from our guy in Tingo María," Henkly said.

"Thanks, Mr. Henkly," Wenton replied.

"Good day, gentlemen," Henkly said with a ring of victory in his voice, then turned and scurried out of the ambassador's office.

"Well, John. This is not what either of us wanted. And please accept my deepest condolences. I know Congressman Kursten was a dear friend of yours."

"Thanks Frank. I appreciate that. Martha and I had just visited him over Christmas," he said, shaking his head. "He invited us over for dinner at his house in Arlington. We hadn't seen each other in several years. We grew up together right outside of Reno. Attended the same schools, all the way through high school. Even played football together. The Garfield Tigers," he said, sighing deeply.

Brinton's eyes began to well up. He took his handkerchief out and dabbed at his eyes before any tears could escape.

"I'm very sorry," Wenton said in a strained voice, barely audible. He knew only too well what it was like to lose a dear friend or family member. He'd just gone through some heavy grieving. His brother had died of a stroke two months before.

He motioned to Brinton to take a seat as he leaned over his desk and pushed the intercom button. "Margaret, would you bring us a couple coffees, please? Both black. Thanks."

"*Sure thing, Mr. Ambassador,*" she replied, and then the intercom buzz went dead.

"You know, Frank, David Kursten was an exceptionally good man," Brinton said.

Ambassador Wenton could see that DCM Brinton was making every effort to dam his emotions and get a grip on himself. "Yes, a really good man. And a damn busy man, though he always made time for his family and friends. When I met with him over Christmas, he was chairing the Senate Judiciary Committee on Crime, Drug Trafficking, and Terrorism. He was also active on a number of other congressional committees. He was one dedicated civil servant, Frank. He'd come to Peru because he felt the DEA's efforts here had produced little. He wanted to see for himself how serious the Peruvian government was about their coca eradication program. That's the only reason he was in that goddamn plane to begin with. To have the government show him evidence, show him the hundreds of hectares of eradicated coca fields they had highlighted in their reports."

The ambassador's secretary entered the office carrying two coffees on a silver tray. She was in her early fifties with short, gray hair cut to shoulder length. She had on a navy skirt, a white silk shirt with a lace collar, and a light blue suit jacket. Careful not to interrupt them, she set the tray down lightly on the table and slipped out as quietly as the draft of air that followed in her wake, closing the door softly behind her.

"Over Christmas, he talked a lot about his efforts to defeat an amendment to the Free Trade Agreement with Peru, an amendment that would result in the Peruvian government banning a number of generic drugs," Brinton continued. "The international pharmaceutical companies were doing their best to see that the amendment was passed. If the amendment passes, that will be an end to many cheap generic drugs entering the Peruvian market. It's all about the big pharms making money. And David said that it looked like the FTA amendment would pass, despite the fact that he was doing all he could to help defeat it. He told me more than two thirds of the senators on the committee would be bought by the pharmaceutical industry."

Wenton sipped his tepid coffee and then set his cup back down on his desk. The thin china cups were too shallow to retain much heat.

"Look John, I'm going to ask the editor of the *Lima Tribune*, Samuel Polsky, to let us send Miss Strand along to Tingo María with his reporter. It would be a good idea to see what she comes up with. I'm not ready to buy into the Shining Path story one hundred percent. I'll arrange to get both of them up there. You've met her, right?"

"Yes, she's the young woman that just arrived from Colombia. Henkly introduced me to her the other day. She writes for Reuters. A real cutie and overflowing with energy. Reminds me of my own daughter. Still young and sparkling with optimism. Not like us old farts," he laughed, relieved to take his thoughts off his friend David Kursten for a moment. "She mentioned she's in Peru writing a piece on the Shining Path and their similarities to the FARC. She strikes me as quite an ambitious young lady."

"I'm sure then that she would jump at the opportunity to go up to the Upper Huallaga. She'd be able to pick up information on the Shining Path there. Interview some of the jungle folk who've had contact with the terrorists. And give us her take on the crash."

"I'd think she'd appreciate the American Embassy's offer to get her up there," Brinton said, an edginess returning to his voice.

Wenton noticed that Brinton looked embarrassed, like maybe he'd been treating the incident a bit too casually, when it was his dear friend who'd perished in the plane crash. Not just some politician.

"I believe Polsky's reporter knows the area well, so he'll be able to show Miss Strand around," Wenton added. "It's imperative to have an alternative view of what happened, not just the Peruvian military's."

The ambassador noticed how his friend had grown sullen. He'd been looking past him out the window, his sad eyes staring off into space.

"I'll do all I can to get to the bottom of this, John. I know that Senator Kursten hated violence and extremism. It would be a shame if his death led to more bloodshed. Let's see what comes up in the next couple days. We'll have more when Miss Strand returns. And Polsky's guy. The State Department will also be sending a team down from Washington to investigate. This will all get sorted out eventually." Wenton smiled weakly, hoping his assurance might lift his friend's mood.

John Brinton returned the smile nodding his head in acknowledgment, though the distant look in his tired, pain swollen eyes belied any genuine conviction.

3

Steve Collins sat at the kitchen bar blowing on his cup, trying to cool the hot, murky liquid. It was Tuesday morning around 10:30 and he was due to pop into the office in half an hour. He had an understanding with his boss that he wouldn't have to show up before 11:00 unless it was something really important, like an early morning interview that couldn't be rescheduled or turned over to the intern. There was usually little to do anyway. Almost half the news Samuel Polsky's paper published was downloaded directly from Reuters or the Associated Press. The *Lima Tribune* was an English language paper with a small circulation, perfect for the expats who eschewed learning Spanish, and perfect for a small-time journalist like Steve with an equally small ambition.

He looked at the headlines on the front page of *El Comercio*, the largest Lima daily. Standard drivel. Bunch of crap about some entertainers from Rio coming to town; an interview with The Black Eyed Peas about a concert scheduled to take place in the *Stadium Monumental*; problems with garbage pickup; talks about a citywide bus strike; and a confrontation between the police and some angry demonstrators in a small mining town in the Andes.

He picked up the TV remote control from the coffee table in the living room and switched on the local news. A sexy woman in a white, low cut baby alpaca sweater was going on excitedly about an accident of some sort. It was hard for his eyes to focus on what she was saying and watch her boobs at the same time. She mentioned something about the Upper Huallaga Valley and then he froze as he heard her say something about a US senator. He immediately turned up the volume.

"*A military search team has been sent to the area. The latest report is that there are no survivors.*"

He almost stumbled over his desk chair as he backed into the kitchen to get his coffee while keeping his eyes glued on the TV.

Before he could pick up the cup, his cellular began buzzing. He walked over to his desk and snatched up his phone.

"*Alo?*"

"Steve?" It was Samuel Polsky, the editor-in-chief and owner of the *Lima Tribune*.

"Yeah, I saw it on the news! Unfucking believable! A US senator!" Steve shot out. "Who's the senator?"

"David Kursten."

"Holy shit. I remember now reading something in *El Comercio* about a US fact finding mission coming to Peru."

"Did the TV reporter say anything about the Shining Path?"

"The Shining Path? No, I mean I don't know. I just turned the TV on when you called. All I heard was something about no survivors. I have the TV on now, but the chick just went to a commercial."

"Look, Ambassador Wenton called. Just got off the phone with him. He's saying that it might not have been a mechanical failure or a pilot error. He has a report coming in from the Peruvian military saying the plane was shot down. His source, a Peruvian colonel in charge of investigating the crash, for what that's worth. The ambassador confided that he's reserving his judgment, and that he'd like our help. He's arranged to get you on an embassy flight to Tingo María first thing tomorrow morning. Apparently he also has some personal interest in the matter."

"So, the ambassador asking you for help? That comes as a surprise," Steve remarked, sipping his coffee.

"Well, we kind of know each other."

"Never pictured you hob-knobbin' with royalty," Steve teased.

"Hardly. He's invited me to a few get-togethers. Not a bad guy, actually. I like his politics. A hell of lot more than a number of assholes at the American Embassy. Speaking of which, before he hung up, he put me through to the new DEA chief, Bill Henkly."

Polsky's words were coming in short breaths like he had just run up a couple of flights of steps.

"Henkly said he'd tell his American Embassy contact in Tingo María to meet you when you arrive."

The small grunts that accompanied Polsky's forced breathing concerned Steve. Last year he'd suffered a minor heart attack. Steve had tried to get him to join Gold's Gym to trim his fat ass down some. He was at least forty pounds overweight, but Polsky just ignored him. Wouldn't leave his desk. He'd have his secretary bring him Dunkin' Donuts in the morning, and for lunch fried empanadas dripping with grease.

"Do I really need an American Embassy contact in Tingo María?"

"Yeah, to get you through to the crash site. Having an embassy rep there will help. You know, Henkly sounded more interested in giving me his opinion about the crash than anything else. Sounds like he has no doubt whatsoever about what happened. He pretty much said that the senator was the target, and that the Shining Path was fulfilling a personal request of the narcos to bring the plane down."

"The narcos?" Steve asked. "You're kidding."

"That's right. According to him, the DEA had assisted the Peruvian authorities in the arrest of Rafael López. So he suspects that Rafael paid the Shining Path handsomely to take care of business. López wanted to send a clear message that if you screw with the wrong people, even if you're a US senator, it's gonna cost. The senator's death, if it's true that López is behind it, will scare the shit out of the Peruvian authorities, and probably stop any extradition proceedings."

"The Shining Path and the narcos? That sounds like warmed over soup. The same crap our government served up in the '90s. The State Department will use the incident to procure more DEA funds to fight the insurgency. It's not about dope. It's about the rebels. They'll try to tie the Shining Path to the FARC. Stories that have been coming out of Colombia, how FARC is financed by drug lords."

Polsky was silent. Steve was wondering what the old boy was thinking. Polsky was hardly naïve.

"Sorry, man, I just don't buy it," Steve continued. "The Shining Path acting as hit men for the narcos? That comes off like a cheap Hollywood thriller."

"Well, Bill Henkly certainly doesn't think so."

As Steve saw it, this Henkly guy's role was to keep the old propaganda machine greased and oiled. And to do whatever was necessary to fund his program. Steve didn't feel like getting into a debate with his boss about the role of the DEA. He'd said enough already, so it would be best to just keep his trap shut.

"Okay, boss, look, do you think the American Embassy can arrange for a copter to transport me to the site? Roads out there where the plane crashed are pretty much non-existent. The Huallaga Valley, that's one huge, untamed jungle."

He paused, reflected for a second on what he was about to say, and then just went for it, firing off his final political salvo. "You know, the right wingers in Washington are going to have a field day with this. They'd be more than happy to napalm all the coca fields and commies in Peru. And then finish up with Colombia, Bolivia, Ecuador, and Venezuela. Get rid of the whole bunch."

"Whatever," Polsky sighed. Steve judged by Polsky's long exasperated sigh that he wasn't keen on listening to his political commentary. "I asked about transporting you to the site. Henkly said the American Embassy doesn't want to risk flying in after what happened. They'll arrange for a jeep with a couple Peruvian escorts."

"Great," Steve replied sarcastically. "Peruvian escorts. How royal of them."

"Hey, look, if you don't wanna go, that's all right with me. I can send Alfonso."

"Alfonso wouldn't know the difference between the Upper Huallaga and Orlando's Gatorland. The chances of him gathering any information of value are about as likely as you giving up donuts. Might as well send your secretary, Elsa."

"Don't be so harsh on the kid," Polsky laughed. "He does all right for an intern. And from your comments, I think sometimes you're just a kid yourself."

"Yeah, well, while I'm gone, have him cover the story on the TV celebrity with the big tits. What's her name? Yeah, Gisela, the one with the libel case against her. Tell him to give her a big squeeze for me and see if those mamas are real."

"Let me decide on the assignments, okay."

Steve realized how he must annoy the old guy. He was always trying to pass off the shit assignment to the intern. And then coming in late to work.

"Whatever you say, boss," he said cheerily, hoping to mollify him. "You know what I need? I need a job like yours. Something real cushy. I could get into just sittin' around the office all day barkin' out orders to my minions."

"Yeah, right," he chuckled. "Like I have a lot of minions to bark out orders to. Anyway, you couldn't handle the stress, son. Staying caged up here all day would drive you crazy."

"Tell me about it. I go stir crazy when I'm in the office more than an hour. Maybe if you'd paint the goddamn place and decorate it some. And clean the frickin' donut crumbs off your desk and floor. Shit, man, you should've become a cop, or opened a Dunkin' Donuts."

"When you're the boss, you can do all those things, okay?"

"Where should I go tomorrow morning?"

"Come to the office around nine o'clock. Hate to ask you to get up so early," he ribbed.

"Can't we make it ten? You know how I have a hard time getting up early," Steve whined, hoping to win Polsky's sympathy. "Also, I have pet responsibilities." Steve looked into the dining

14

room where Arty, his blowfish, was sleeping at the bottom of the fish bowl.

"What pet?" Polsky grumbled.

"Arty, my fish buddy."

"Get out of here. If you're late, you're really gonna piss me off."

"I'll be there at nine," Steve grumbled.

"Look, I have to go. You get to bed early, okay. Forget the girl chasing and bar hopping, son," he said in this paternal voice he often used with Steve. Steve didn't mind really. There wasn't much of a paternal voice around when he was growing up. His father, a mechanic, had split when he was just a kid. He could barely remember the tall, thin, chain-smoking figure that smelled of Lucky Strikes and car grease.

"Okay boss, early to bed it will be," though he knew the odds against that happening. He'd already planned to meet his buddy Gerardo that night. "See you tomorrow bright and early."

"Remember nine o'clock, not ten," Polsky warned again.

"Over and out, boss," he said, and then hung up the phone.

Steve touched his forehead. It was damp with sweat. He'd suddenly developed a slight headache and his stomach felt a little queasy as well. Maybe it was the black coffee on an empty stomach, although he knew better.

He went to the bathroom, opened the medicine cabinet and pulled out a bottle of Pepto-Bismol. After giving it a good shake, he removed the cap and took a healthy swig of the pink gooey liquid. He hoped that would do the trick.

The idea of returning to the Upper Huallaga after all these years had definitely unsettled his stomach. Although Polsky had been joking, maybe he should've sent the kid. Steve just didn't feel ready to go back there.

As he entered the living room, he noticed the same sexy news lady was now interviewing a TV soap opera star, some young kid with greased back hair and a broad smile like you see in toothpaste commercials. He thought of his own teeth. Maybe he'd get them whitened like the soap opera kid. No, on second thought they were just fine. He needed a drink. Perhaps that would put his stomach nerves to sleep, though hard liquor this early was not what the doctor would prescribe. But what the hell. He needed chill out.

He grabbed the Bacardi from the wall cabinet and then went into the kitchen and took a bottle of Coke from the refrigerator and a few ice cubes from the freezer. As he stirred the drink, he watched the ice cubes swirl round and round like old memories colliding with the present, reminding him how he'd ended up working for a second rate newspaper in a remote corner of the earth. He'd wasted a good part of his professional life, if you could call it that, writing pieces on cuisine or travel, or translating articles from the local papers into English for the *Lima Tribune*. Occasionally he'd interview a government minister, write a special on a Peruvian banker or politician, a textile merchant, or the CEO of a mining enterprise or international firm. For over a decade now, that was about as close as he came to writing anything substantial. It didn't use to be that way, but that was a long time ago. Another life.

Now his boss was asking him to return to the jungle and cover a blockbuster story about a dead US senator. And maybe about the Shining Path rebels. As he thought about returning to the Huallaga Valley, he wanted to believe he'd paid his dues, but maybe that was the problem. He hadn't, and this was an opportunity for him to do just that. Not that he could ever make things right, but this time telling the truth was more important than ever.

He took a heavy swig of his drink and felt the burning sensation as it slid down his throat. There are many ways to seek escape, he reflected. He had sought it by distancing himself from a place that had changed his life forever. It had been over two decades since he'd visited the Huallaga Valley. But distancing himself hadn't worked. If there was one thing he had learned, it was that the shortest distance between two points is not a straight line. It's memory, a psychic force that defies physics, dissolves time and distance, and makes an event as starkly real and immediate as though it was happening right here and now. Alcohol could momentarily blur the edges of memory, but it was no escape. No you had to confront your demons to conquer them. Tomorrow might just give him that chance. Instead of feeling dread about returning to the Huallaga Valley, he needed to feel that fate was offering him a onetime deal that he would be a fool not to take advantage of. But how could he really be sure? Nothing was certain, except this feeling deep down inside him that his best weapon was atonement.

4

It was almost midnight when Steve arrived at Rosita's, a popular *salsodromo* in the district of Rimac, an infamously poor area of Lima seldom visited by foreigners. The cab pulled up in front of a late 19th century colonial mansion with a crumbling, blue pastel facade. An old Spanish balcony with crisscrossing lattice in desperate need of paint jutted out over the entrance. The left side of the balcony sagged, threatening to detach itself from the building.

Inside, the *salsodromo* was immense. The interior walls of this enormous old building had been removed. The place was like a huge gutted whale, and before the night ended would smell like one. The toilets would be plugged and unflushable. The air would reek of spilled beer, greasy food, and sweat. For Steve, these were small drawbacks, more than compensated for by the vibrant atmosphere created by the extraordinary salsa bands that played here.

As soon as he walked in, he saw Gerardo sitting at one of the numerous oblong wooden tables arranged around a large, brightly lit dance floor.

"Hey, how goes it?" Steve asked while eyeing the two girls sitting on each side of Gerardo.

"Great, amigo. Happy to see you made it. I was beginning to think you'd drowned while crossing the Rimac."

"Pretty tough to drown yourself in a dry sewer bed, dude. You girls speak English?" Steve noticed the two young women giving him the once over, probably not understanding a word of what had just passed between him and Gerardo.

"Yes, I speak English. But not good English. Just a leetle English," the small, darker one said with a sexy smile while running her hand playfully through Gerardo's thick black hair. Her companion, a light-skinned *mestizo*, about a head taller than her friend, wore a tight polyester blouse with a bright flower pattern straining to hold in her womanly treasures. She smiled politely at Steve and then quickly returned her gaze to a young man about her own age who'd been checking her out over the shoulder of his dance partner.

"You from *Estados Unidos*? I mean the United States?" Gerardo's girl asked giggling, apparently feeling silly and awkward trying to speak a language in which she possessed only a meager vocabulary. "I have uncle in Miami."

"Miami? Great," Steve replied, not the least bit interested. It seemed that every Peruvian on the planet had a relative in Miami. And every one of them was eager to boast about it.

"Gerardo, what do you say we get a round of drinks?" While he said this he ran his hand lightly underneath the chin of the taller girl. She had momentarily lost interest in the guy on the dance floor who'd been ogling her. She now fixed her eyes intently on Steve.

"*Flaco, tres cervezas, por favor*!" Steve shouted to the waiter as he moved his shoulders to the wave of music that crashed over them like a tsunami. The brass section of the band had just stepped it up. The trumpets threatened to blow the roof off the building. Steve loved the sheer power and majesty of the horns. As he bumped his shoulder against the girl's shoulder, she bumped back. He then raised his hands above his head and started clapping. The short girl joined in, while Gerardo pounded the table trying to follow the feverish rhythm of the congas.

"What's your name?" Steve asked. She had bright obsidian eyes that trapped the light and sparkled.

"Carla." She slid closer to him, pressing her leg against his.

"*Te gusta la música?*" he asked, resting his shoulder against her soft dark skin.

"I like," she said. "Music good."

As one of the trumpet players broke free from the rest of the horn section, the others fell back and became the underpinning for his solo. His notes soared so high that Steve could imagine them splitting the roof in two. In stratospheric reaches, Maynard Ferguson had nothing over him.

He was thinking about pulling Carla onto the dance floor when he was struck dumb by a lovely woman trying to follow the moves of her Latino dancing companion. Her awkwardness gave her away. She was definitely a *gringa*. Smiling broadly and looking like she was trying as hard as she could not to burst out laughing, she struggled to follow the moves of her short, stocky partner. He was going crazy on her, executing lightening quick passes and shaking his shoulders like he had a bad case of Saint Vitus's dance. The guy was definitely more energy than finesse, a cocky little show-off trying to impress this charming woman. She laughed hysterically every time she tried to imitate one of his exaggerated moves.

When the song ended, she looked totally spent. But not the salsa king. He was hot to trot. With sweat streaming down his forehead, and his shirt opened advertising his hairy chest, he tried his best to persuade her to stay on the dance floor. As the band struck up a new song, she politely smiled and shook her head no. He repeated something to her, but she just held up her hands and shrugged, apparently not understanding much of his Spanish, or perhaps not hearing him clearly above the loud music. He finally gave up and they exchanged kisses on the cheek. As she left the dance floor, she walked past Steve's table, made subtle eye contact with him, and then disappeared in the dimly lit space a few tables behind him.

"I'll be right back," he half mumbled to Carla. She had watched him staring at the *gringa,* and when he said he'd be right back, she just turned her head away from him like she could care less.

"Hey, man, where you off to?" Gerardo asked.

"Give me a minute."

"Sure. Don't keep this *bella chica* waitin'." Then turning back to the girl he'd been chatting up, he began playing with her long dark curls.

Steve had already set off trying to find his way in the dim lighting, pulled along in the wake of this classy woman who had just glided by his table. When he caught sight of her two tables back, he hurried toward her before she could sit down.

"Hey, you dance well, you know," he said, lightly touching her arm. She turned around and then smiled as though she had just run into an old acquaintance. Her large dark eyes held Steve spellbound. She was even more beautiful up close.

"Yeah, sure," she laughed. "I must've looked real spastic out there." Her voice reminded Steve of the light tinkle of wind chimes.

"You weren't doing bad at all, not for a *gringa.*" As he said this, his eyes took in her black satin dress highlighting her sensuous curves. He had difficulty keeping his eyes from going into roving mode.

"*Gringa?*" she burst out laughing. "You don't exactly look like Julio Iglesias."

"No, but I can dance like him. Wanna see?"

"He's a singer."

"Yeah, well I can do that as well. Check this out.

"*Abrazame, y no me digas nada. Solo abrazame. Me basta tu mirada para comprender!*" He sang in the lowest tenor he could, leaning into her, his hand over his heart, with this comically exaggerated love struck look in his eyes. A real vaudeville act. It looked like any moment he might drop to one knee and go into singing Al Jolsen's "Mamie."

"Gee, I'm impressed."

Steve noticed her pursing her beautiful lips to restrain her laughter as she lightly applauded his performance.

"So will that get me a dance? I promise not to pull any hotshot movements on you, like that dude you were dancing."

"That dude!" she laughed. "Now aren't you the hip one."

"Well, come on now. Go easy on me. If you think saying 'dude' makes me sound hip, then okay. I accept. Nothing wrong with being hip." He really enjoyed her spirited mood. "So how about that dance?"

His timing was perfect. At that exact moment the band decided to slow things down and play *"Burbujas de Amor."*

She arched her eyebrow in the form of a question mark and looked straight into his pleading eyes.

He waited in anticipation while a coy smile played on her lips, totally disarming him.

"Well?" he asked.

"Yeah, sure. Why not," she said, holding her hand out to him.

Steve didn't waste a second. He took her hand and gently pulled her out onto the crowded dance floor.

"I love this song," he said.

God, she was beautiful. Looking at her lovely face made him think of some of his favorite lines from the Bard.

> Oh, *she doth teach the torches to burn bright!*
> *It seems* she *hangs upon the cheek of night.*
> *Like a rich jewel in an Ethiope's ear.*
> *Beauty too rich for use*
> *For earth to dear.*

Shit, now he truly understood what those lines meant. He had living proof that such a thing could be.

It pleased him when he pulled her closer to him and felt no resistance.

"Juan Luis Guerra, right? They used to play this song on the radio all the time in Colombia."

"Colombia? So, what do we have here, a world traveler? How long you in Lima?" He was hoping her answer would be "forever and a day."

"A very short time, unfortunately. I wish I had more time to see this enchanting country," she sighed and then smiled. "I've heard such wonderful things about Peru."

"It's an incredible place. How long's a very short time?"

"Just a few more days."

"So, have you seen much of Lima?" He was just stalling for time, wanting to keep her close to him, to feel her breasts nuzzled against his chest and smell the lovely fragrance of her hair.

"Not a whole lot. I noticed Lima has a lot of the poverty. That's a bit disturbing. Reminds me a lot of Bogotá." She pushed back a little, letting him know that there were certain boundaries that needed to be respected.

"It has its attractions, though." He relaxed his hold, though it felt so wonderful to feel her soft body pressed against his. He hoped he hadn't given her the wrong idea, whatever that meant.

"Attractions? I've never thought of poverty as being attractive."

"Yeah, well, some see it as attractive. Makes them feel like the chosen few. Like Hitler's Nazis must have felt when they swept over Eastern Europe."

"Nazis? Get out of here. How did you come up with that crazy idea?"

"Well, the way I see it, some gringos down here feel a bit like the Nazis must have felt at the apex of Hitler's power, before his Aryan fiasco fell apart."

"Like a Nazi? That's a pretty weird thing to say."

By the look on her face, he could see that she wasn't sure what to make of him. Sometimes he wasn't sure what to make of him. He often surprised himself. Like right now. Why was he making himself so unattractive? So fucking retarded sounding. Maybe it was nerves. When he got nervous, he had this urge to run off at the mouth.

"I hope you aren't a skinhead," she laughed. "Is that a wig you have on?" She leaned back and pretended to examine his curly brown hair.

"No, that's real hair." He felt suddenly relieved that she wasn't too spooked by his rant. He needed to explain himself.

"I just meant that it's easy for those who have much more than others to become less critical of economic realities and invent or embrace world views that justify privilege. If you stay around here long enough, you'll see what I mean. So many gringos become just like their *pituco* friends, believing that success has to do with being special, and none of the poor folk have that special whatever it is."

"*Pituco?*"

"Yeah, Peruvian slang for the spoiled, pretentious rich, and their wannabe friends."

"Are you always so cheery?" she teased, as the waltz ended.

"Sorry if I sounded cynical. Whenever I wax political, I usually get that way. Most of the time I'm happy and frivolous, so don't worry, it's a passing thing."

"Hey, how about some fresh air?" she asked, tugging playfully on his arm, pulling him in the direction of the front door. "Maybe that would cheer you up."

"Yeah, I think that's a jewel of an idea. Let me say goodbye to my friends first. By the way, if you really want to get some fresh air, my apartment has a beautiful balcony view of the ocean and the air couldn't be fresher. Lots of fresh air there."

She smiled and looked at her watch, which gave his eyes a split second to wander from hers down to her low cut dress. A few beads of sweat had formed at the bottom of her neck. One of the larger, heavier beads broke free and began coursing down the valley between the lovely slopes of her partially exposed breasts.

"Well…" she said, and then paused for a second as she looked into his eyes with this curious fascination and seduction that totally transfixed him. "Where is your apartment?"

"In Miraflores, on the boardwalk near the Marriott."

"Why we're neighbors. I'm staying at the Hotel Americas, just a few blocks from the Marriott. Okay, buddy boy. I'll accept your offer, as long as you promise to be a gentleman. And lay off that Nazi nonsense."

"It's a promise." How could he not be a gentleman around this lovely lady? Was he awake or dreaming? Everything seemed to be happening too fast to be real.

"Say goodbye to your friends and meet me at the door, then," she said, taking her sweater from the bench.

"Will do!"

Back at the table, Gerardo looked like he was in bachelor heaven. Sitting between the two girls, his arms around both of them, positioned perfectly to cop a feel, he replenished their glasses as the three of them laughed and carried on.

"Hey, *compadre*! What's happening?" he yelled out as he saw Steve approach. "Your *chica* was wondering where you disappeared," he said gesturing to Carla, who immediately looked away, pretending to ignore Steve. "I've been takin' up the slack for you, trying to keep her company."

"Yeah, I can see. Sorry for making you suffer. Look, amigo, I have to run." Steve reached into his pocket and took out a wrinkled wad of Peruvian *soles*. "Here buy yourself and the girls another round on me. Later, man."

"Hey Steve, you can't leave now," Gerardo moaned.

"Sorry. Got to go. I'll call you later." He leaned over and kissed Gerardo's girl on the cheek and then turned to Carla. She smiled this big fake smile as he kissed her on the cheek, after which her lips quickly formed into a pout.

Outside the *salsodromo*, Steve saw two taxis parked next to the curb directly across the street. The night air was thick and damp. A heavy fog covered the old neighborhood casting a gauzy haze over everything and making it difficult to see farther than a few meters.

Two taxi drivers, laughing while leaning against the fender of one of the cabs, stopped suddenly when they saw two gringos step through the fog toward them. At the same time two ragged street kids emerged from nowhere and immediately approached Steve. They were young kids, maybe ten or eleven years old at most.

"Por favor, mister, una propina," the taller of the two said. His thick, black hair was matted down on the top of his head. Starched by urban grime, the untrimmed hair over his ears stuck out to the sides like ruffled pigeon wings. When he looked up at Steve, the streetlight above cast a soft light on his round dark face, revealing a toothy, heartwarming smile.

Steve reached into his pocket and pulled out a couple shiny *soles* and slapped them into the boy's small hand. "*Esto es para los dos,*" he said in this paternal voice, making it clear that the money was for both of them.

Feigning a businesslike indifference, the two cabbies watched as Steve and the young woman approached them. They acted like they had all the time in the world, and that a *sol* here or there in their pockets was of little importance, especially for two prosperous guys like themselves who owned their own taxis.

"*Buenas noches*! What would you charge to take us to Miraflores?" Steve asked in a business-like tone, hoping to dispel the idea that he and the girl were just a couple of rich gringos.

"*Buenas noches*! To Miraflores? one of the taxi drivers asked, scratching his chin. That would cost fifty *soles*."

"Hey, *flaco*," Steve laughed, knowing full well the cabbie had asked twice the going fare. "I'm no tourist. I live in Lima. I'm a resident. Twenty-five *soles*. Okay?"

"Okay, Mister!"

"I can see you know your way around. How long did it take to acquire your level of street savvy? I'm jealous, she said."

"With your beauty, mundane skills like mine are superfluous. All you have to do is smile that charming smile of yours and they'll take you anywhere, free of charge." He wasn't bullshitting her either. Her charm had certainly worked its mojo on him.

The taxi driver opened the back door of the cab, and Steve waited for her to climb in before he scrunched in beside her. Sitting next to her, it suddenly struck him that he didn't even know this lovely woman's name.

"By the way, my name's Steve, Steve Collins. And yours?"

"Jennifer, and not Jenny please."

"No, I like Jennifer. Jenny is a little girl's name. And you're no little girl," he joked, "though you do have an innocent sweetness about you."

"Don't think to gain anything by flattery, buddy-boy, though I guess it doesn't hurt your chances either."

In the early morning hours with few cars on the streets, the taxi took only about twenty minutes to reach Steve's apartment. Inside the cramped confines of the taxi, Steve noticed how his clothes reeked of cigarette smoke. In Rimac smoking bans were never enforced. The police had other concerns. Across the river, it wasn't cancer that killed you. He couldn't wait to jump in the shower and scrub the nasty smell out of his hair. After a few drinks and a little coaxing, maybe he could talk Jennifer into joining him. He was feeling like this could be his lucky night.

"*Buenas noches*, Senior Collins." Ricardo, the doorman, had seen the taxi pull up out front and was at the door rubbing the sleep out of his eyes before Steve could buzz him. He'd probably fallen asleep while watching a program on the tiny portable TV resting on the counter top.

Jennifer stood behind Steve studying some replicas of Pre-Incan pottery displayed in a glassed-in shelf near the front door.

"Ready to see that beautiful view?" he asked.

She was totally absorbed in the details of the pottery. "Moche or Chimú?"

"I wouldn't know. You an archeologist?"

"No, just read about the two cultures in a travel book I picked up." Then turning from the pottery and looking at Steve, "Okay, let's go see that view you were bragging about." Under the florescent lights in the lobby, her eyes seemed to glow even brighter.

As soon as Steve opened the door to his apartment, he pointed in the direction of the balcony. "There she is," he said. "Check it out."

She stepped across the living room and pushed open the sliding glass doors.

"Wow! It is a beautiful view. That lit up cross over there. It must be huge."

"Yep. That's over in Chorrillos. Jesus looking out for his folks there."

"Geez, it sure is nippy out here." She adjusted her sweater, pulling the collar up around her neck and drawing the unbuttoned front together.

"Would you like a drink?"

"Sure."

She stepped from the breezy balcony back into the living room. Her eyes sparkled as she spread her arms out in a gesture that was meant to include the entire apartment in her remark. "This is really a great place you have here! Congratulations. And you were right. You do have a marvelous view from the balcony."

She sauntered over to a small table next to the credenza where Steve had his liquor cabinet and his stereo and CDs. Rummaging through a stack of CDs, she chose, *Reunion Blues*, one of Milt Jackson's classic recordings with Oscar Peterson on piano and Milt on vibes.

"You like Jazz?" Steve asked, taking the disk from her and sliding it into the player.

"Grew up on it. My mother played the jazz clarinet."

"So, Milt Jackson? Do you get good vibes from him?"

"You can do better than that now," she said, laughing at the silly pun.

He suddenly felt like some childish school boy trying to impress this sophisticated young lady with his adolescent wit. He could feel the blood rushing to his face.

"How about a margarita? Yes, definitely, a margarita. You look like a margarita person."

"A margarita person? So you read minds, do you? I do like margaritas, though I doubt you divined that."

"No, I was just guessing."

"I bet it's a popular drink among all the young women folk you invite up here for the view," she teased.

"Let's just say, I know what beautiful women like you like."

"Oh, do you now?" she laughed.

"When it comes to drinks, that is. Go ahead a make yourself comfortable while I fix your drink."

While he made her margarita, he noticed her flipping through the pages of an old issue of *The Atlantic* he had left on the side table near the sofa. How stupid of him. In the afternoon, after Polsky called, he got loaded and dug out the old issue he had stuffed away in the closet. Why he still kept it after all these years would take a shrink to figure out. Discussing his past fiasco at *The Atlantic* really wasn't the kind of conversation he wanted to have with this gorgeous woman.

"Wow, you are full of surprises. 'A Daring Interview with *Sendero Luminoso*, Peru's Fanatical Terrorist Group,'" she read aloud. "So you wrote for *The Atlantic*?"

"Yeah, that was centuries ago, or so it seems."

He handed her the margarita he'd prepared for her.

"Before I decided to move up to a job at the *Lima Tribune*. Some would see that as a step down, but not me. My passion's writing articles about Peruvian cuisine and doing interviews with Peruvian soap opera stars."

"Come on now," she said. "You're jesting? There's got to be a story here. I'm dying to hear it."

"Yeah, there's a story alright. Suffice it to say, not a very pretty one, and one I'd rather not talk about, if that's okay with you."

"If you say so. I won't pry," she said turning her lower lip up in mock disappointment. She set the magazine down on the side table and walked back to the balcony.

"I appreciate that," he said as he followed her outside. He sidled up next to her as she leaned over the rail breathing in the damp, salty air. "I don't know about you, but the ocean always has this calming effect on me."

"Yeah, I know what you mean. I love the ocean too. You know you would've never gotten me up here if you hadn't mentioned the ocean view."

"I thought my charm was enough to do the trick."

"Going off about Nazis is hardly any way to win a young woman's heart, or even make her peripherally interested. It's a good way to scare the crap out her though. Especially if you just met. Some advice for the future."

"Well, thanks. I'll try to remember your advice. To a beautiful night," he said, raising his glass to hers.

"Yes, to a beautiful night. But I'm afraid it's going to have to be a short one." She clicked her glass against his and then raised it to her lips and took a few sips.

"A short one? You're kidding me."

"Nope. Sorry," she said with a mock frown.

"Sure I can't convince you to stay a little longer?"

"Afraid not. Tomorrow's a busy day, but I really enjoyed myself tonight. I'm glad I decided to brave it and go to Rosita's. I asked a cabby the other day where to go to hear some good salsa, and he said Rosita's. When I crossed the river into Rimac, I have to say, I was a bit worried."

"Yeah, Rosita's is a great place, but Rimac is the pits."

"By the way, thanks for the taxi ride back."

"My pleasure."

"And the margarita. You do make great ones."

"Sure you don't want another one?"

No, I need to scoot," she said with a bewitching smile that nearly bought Steve to tears knowing he wouldn't be able to convince her to stay. "I really enjoyed the invite, but I do need to get up early."

She took a sip of her drink and then stepped back into the living room.

"I have a wonderful alarm clock."

"Yes, I'm sure you do," she laughed. "I'll bet it rarely fails to get the girls up and into a taxi before you're off to work," she taunted.

"I hate to shatter your illusions about bachelors, but...it's just that..."

"I know...It's not that way with you," she grinned.

"No, I wasn't going to say that at all. I was about to say it doesn't always get them up."

"Thanks for the drink, Steve, she replied, shaking her head in disbelief at his boldness. "I do really have to go. And it has been a pleasure." She touched the side of her glass against his and then set it down on the counter.

"Is there any chance we could get together again? Before you're out of here?" He was desperate to see her one more time, though she said she'd only be in town for a few more days. Maybe that was part of what attracted him to her. The possibility of a short term romance without commitments. He hoped not. He didn't want to believe that his relationships with the opposite sex were becoming that pathetic, but based on his dating record the last few years, the thought might be worth considering.

Jennifer grabbed her pocketbook from the sofa, took a pen and a small note pad out, and wrote out her number. "Give me a call," she said almost in a whisper. "And thanks again for inviting me up." She leaned forward and gave him a light kiss on the cheek and then turned to leave.

"Let me get you a cab," he said as he opened the hall door.

"No, that won't be necessary. I'm only a few blocks away."

"I can walk you to your hotel, if you like."

"No, that's okay. I'm a big girl. I'll be fine."

"You sure?" he asked pleadingly.

"I'm sure." Then she smiled one last time and said, "Do call me. Maybe we can go out for a coffee."

"Will do. *Buenas noches.*"

"*Buenas noches,*" she said as she walked across the hall and pressed the elevator button. Steve couldn't take his eyes off her as he waited for the elevator's familiar ping.

"Bye!" she called out and waved as the stainless steel doors opened and she stepped in.

Shit, he nearly said aloud, after she'd disappeared behind the shiny doors. He suddenly realized that he was off to the jungle tomorrow and by the time he returned she'd most likely be gone. What crap luck. Glumly he accepted the fact he'd probably never see her again and slowly closed his door.

When he turned around the first thing that caught his attention was the old copy of *The Atlantic* lying on the coffee table. He walked over, picked it up, and held its thin pages between his finger and thumb. Feeling the magazine's flimsiness, he reflected on how a six-page article could so alter a person's life. The thought made his stomach tighten.

Silly as it might sound, after the fraud was discovered, he couldn't get Mr. Carter, his high school journalism teacher, out of his mind. He kept recalling Mr. Carter's talk on the ethics of journalism and the journalist's responsibility to tell the truth and keep his own opinion out of the story. *"A good journalist must avoid sensationalism and yellow journalism! And get his or her facts straight! Must tell the truth, with accuracy and precision, but most of all with honesty."* What had Mr. Carter thought about him when the news broke? The story had made the front page of the *New York Times*, for Christ's sake. Here was his star pupil. A kid he had been so proud of. And now a super fraud.

He dropped the magazine in the trash basket under the kitchen sink and then turned the living room light off. He'd carried the fucking magazine around too long as it was.

As he stood there in the darkness, a cold shiver passed through him. He'd left the balcony doors open and he could feel the chilly, early morning air brush against his skin. All these years, the magazine article had been like an albatross around his neck. It was time to cut the bird loose. He'd never, ever wanted again to return to the Upper Huallaga. He'd avoided it like the plague, and now he would be going back. Maybe tossing the magazine in the trash was nothing more than a symbolic act, but he preferred to think of it as a first step. If he couldn't change the past, he would at least refuse to let it destroy him. But that meant confronting it. Returning to the Huallaga Valley might just be a blessing in disguise.

5

Steve heard a noise in the distance like an electric drill being turned on and off causing his foggy, pre-conscious thoughts to land him in his dentist's office. Right when the drill was about to auger its way into his molar, he realized the fraud his mind had committed. He rolled over in bed and snatched the vibrating culprit from the night stand. His first impulse was to smash the damn clock on the floor. Then in a flash it dawned on him that he was supposed to be in Samuel Polsky's office in less than ten minutes.

He sprang out of bed, stumbled into the bathroom and turned on the shower. Two minutes later, after toweling himself down, he rushed back into the bedroom, grabbed some underwear and socks from the chest of drawers, extra shirts and pants from the closet, and crammed them into his duffel bag. Hair dripping, he swept his camera from the top of his dresser and hurried out the door, leaving behind a trail of steam and a faint smell of soap.

Fifteen minutes later and short of breath, he arrived at the *Lima Tribune*. The newspaper's office was located on a narrow street off Avenida Larco, Miraflores's main drag. With his duffel slung over his right shoulder and his camera over his left, he rushed into the entrance of the building, nodded to the doorman, and darted up the stairs. He was about ten minutes late.

When he opened the door to Polsky's office, his heart stopped. There, sitting in a chair in front of Polsky's desk was Jennifer.

Polsky eyes locked on Steve. "Shit! Can't you ever be on time! I told you nine o'clock."

"Sorry. Damned alarm clock." He looked at Jennifer and grinned sheepishly. "It usually doesn't fail."

Polsky rose and waddled from behind his desk. "I'd like you to meet the young lady that'll be accompanying you." He nodded his head at Jennifer. "Ms. Strand, from Reuters. She'll be going with you to the crash site."

Lima's a small world as far as bumping into expats goes, Steve thought, but this felt too much like synchronicity. He didn't believe in that crap, but seeing her sitting there in Polsky's office made him a true believer.

"Hello Steve," Jennifer said, her beautiful, dark eyes smiling up at him. "It's a pleasure to meet you."

"Good! Enough of formal introductions!" Polsky exclaimed. "You two can get acquainted later. You need to head out to the airport now. Mr. Henkly has arranged with the Peruvian Air Force to fly you two up to Tingo María. He said he'd meet you at Gate B before you board."

All in a huff, Polsky shoved the office door open and pushed Steve out into the hall.

Steve glanced back at Jennifer. She was doing her utmost to suppress bursting out laughing. The old guy had worked himself into a frenzy. He was really too much. His forehead was covered in sweat, and he had telltale sugar marks caked at the corners of his mouth from the donuts he'd already polished off.

Polsky turned to Jennifer. "You two need to watch yourself up there. The place could be swarming with *Senderistas*."

"Hey, don't scare her, boss!"

"But they're probably the least of your worries. It's this fellow here I'd watch out for."

"What? Come on, now. You know I'm a perfect gentleman," Steve beamed, but at the same time felt a little embarrassed, which surprised him. "She'll be fine with me."

Polsky screwed his eyes up and muttered, "Sure," and then paused before exploding in an uncontrollable fit of laughter. For a moment, Steve thought the old boy might've overdone it. In the middle of his howling fit, he started coughing. Then suddenly began choking. Jennifer looked alarmed. When the coughing fit finally subsided, and he looked like he'd recovered, Steve put his arm over his shoulder and walked him over to the top of stairs.

"You okay?" Steve asked.

"Yeah, I'll be all right," he said, his face two shades redder than normal and his eyes tear-brimmed. "Now you two get off to the airport before you miss your plane."

"We're off," Steve replied, and then headed down the stairs, his duffel bag over his shoulder and his camera in his hand. "You have any bags?" He saw that Jennifer only had her purse with her.

"Yes, they're down in the lobby. I left them with the doorman."

As he stepped out into the street to flag a taxi, he thought about Polsky and promised himself that he'd convince Samuel to buy a gym membership. Hell, if he had to, he'd even sign up with him when he got back. He'd hate to lose the old guy.

Shortly after lifting off from Lima, they were flying over the Cordillera Blanca, the front range of the Andes. The ride had been relatively smooth. In about thirty minutes they would begin their descent into Tingo María. As the plane broke through the clouds, banana and sugar cane crops came sharply into view. The flat jungle landscape they'd been flying over had now converted into valleys, ridges, and plateaus, not unlike a scene from *Jurassic Park*. It wouldn't be out of place to see a Pterosaur fly by, Steve mused.

Even though it had been years since he'd been to Tingo María, he doubted much had changed. He suspected the outlying roads were still dirt and hardly passable, especially after a hard rain. The larger Upper Huallaga region, which included Tingo María, was no doubt tamer than a couple decades ago when it was a serpent's nest of guerilla activity and cocaine trafficking. He imagined the locals now were mostly poor *campesinos* and small shop owners, with a few drug dealers tossed in. Recently he'd heard about some Shining Path activity. Just a few weeks ago he'd read in *IDL Reporteros* about a confrontation between a military convoy and a dozen or so Shining Path rebels. Apparently it was a relatively small, insignificant incident that didn't merit much national or international press attention.

Although not of much interest to most tourists, the Upper Huallaga did attract a handful of adventurous foreigners, mostly low-budget backpackers that had never traveled outside of their own countries and longed to visit the heart of the Amazon. For those wishing to throw caution to the wind and experiment with drugs, this remote part of the jungle was the ideal place. Something akin to Conrad's heart of darkness, a place where one's soul could go perfectly mad. To assist, there were shamans enough to go around, long-haired, necklace clad, half-naked faith healers mixing up rare concoctions guaranteed to produce the ultimate trip.

Also drawn to the Huallaga was an occasional wannabe drug smuggler, usually young, naïve, and from Europe, looking for a quick way to make a pile of Euros. Or an adventurous naturalist studying the flora and fauna, dreaming of discovering a new species. Maybe even a one or two intrepid anthropologists, followers of Margaret Mead or Claude Lévi-Strauss, in pursuit of a primitive tribe to study, or join. At one point in his life, Steve had jokingly thought about following in their footsteps. Not studying primitive tribes, just joining one. The ultimate escape.

For those who did not wish to drift too far outside the thin veil of civilized life but wanted to experience a taste of jungle living, Tingo María would most likely not be their first choice. For tourism, it and most of the Huallaga Valley were off the map. Even though not described as such in the travel guides, Tingo was as a dirty, rundown town of about 55,000 inhabitants, most of them living in abject poverty and stewing under an intense tropical sun.

Jennifer sat across from Steve in a small seat next to an equally small window. The plane, a noisy de Havilland Twin Otter, at least fifteen years old, bounced through the clouds striking occasional air pockets and jolting the plane sufficiently to lift them a few inches in their seats. Although they were only separated by an aisle slightly wider than Steve's narrow hips, they had to nearly scream to hear each other over the drone of the twin engines.

"So what's your deal with Reuters?" Steve yelled out leaning across the aisle.

"At the moment, not much. Just finishing up a piece on the elections in Colombia. In the meantime, I'm working on a feature for *Harpers* on terrorism and drug trafficking in the Upper Huallaga. I've finished a first draft on Colombia's FARC rebels, and so I thought that it would be a good idea to visit Peru for a couple of weeks and maybe expand the article to include the whole region."

"Getting too close to the action can be dangerous. But I guess you know that. Out here it can be like the Wild West."

"Well, Wild Bill, I don't plan to spend a whole lot of time in the Wild West."

Steve just smiled without replying.

"My plan was to visit a coca producing area. One close to where the rebels have been operating, and interview this drug lord. I was planning on taking a bus to the jungle. Then the plane crashed yesterday killing a US senator. I heard on CNN a rumor about possible terrorist involvement. All of this happening right while I'm here in Lima."

"Polsky said that it was Bill Henkly's idea that you tag along." Steve couldn't see the connection between *Harpers* and the American Embassy in Peru.

"I didn't hear that!" Jennifer yelled back, putting her hand to her ear.

"Polsky kind of hinted that it was Henkly's idea that you tag along," Steve repeated, notching his voice up an octave.

"Tag along?"

"His words, not mine."

Jennifer loosened her seatbelt so she could move in closer to Steve in order to be heard. "Last night at your apartment when I told you I had a busy schedule the following day, I wasn't kidding.

I had an eight o'clock appointment with Mr. Henkly. He asked me about my visit to Lima, and I told him I was planning to write a piece on narco-terrorism and a drug trafficker named Rafael López. López is apparently operating in the same area near where the plane went down.

"And?"

"Well, Mr. Henkly said he would be happy to get me to the crash site, if…, she paused for a couple of seconds. "If I would share any information with him I planned to use, either in my article or about the plane crash. Share it, before I released it."

"So you agreed to his ridiculous *quid pro quo*?" Steve asked without thinking about how she would take his remark.

She was about to answer when the small door between the cabin and passenger compartment opened and the co-pilot called out, "Prepare for landing."

She slid over into her seat and readjusted her seatbelt. Then she took a Baltimore Orioles baseball cap out of her bag and pulled it down over her long black hair.

"We'll talk later," she yelled, glancing over at Steve. She grabbed her purse from under the seat in front of her, withdrew a small round compact, studied her face for a few seconds, snapped the compact shut, and then replaced it in her purse.

We'll talk later, Steve reflected. What would be the point? Why go there? He knew how the State Department worked, and if she wanted to go along with them, why interfere? His job was to check out the crash and write it up. Truthfully. No politics involved. Just straightforward, clean, honest journalism.

As the plane came to a stop, Steve watched out the small side window while the props stirred up blasts of dust. He could make out two Peruvian soldiers approaching the plane accompanied by a tall, well-dressed American in his mid-thirties.

The copilot opened the side door of the plane and motioned above the noise of the engines to Jennifer and Steve to step down. Jennifer grabbed the bill of her Orioles cap as gusts of hot air from the props fought to lift it.

The American and a Peruvian officer in his early fifties with graying sideburns stepped forward to greet them. The American, dressed in a gray suit with a red and blue tie, looked to be about six two. He had a neatly trimmed moustache and short sideburns and looked to Steve like a typically well-groomed government official with a stick up his ass. His dark sunglasses made it impossible to see his eyes.

"Hello, I'm Frank Pierce," the American said, extending his hand to Steve.

"Steve Collins. Pleased to meet you."

"And I'm Jennifer Strand. My pleasure," she said as they shook hands.

"As you may have guessed, I'm the American Embassy representative assigned to Tingo María. This is Colonel Juan Luis Montero, the head of the military operation here." He nodded to the smiling gentleman standing at his side.

The colonel gripped Steve's hand forcefully and gave it a solid shake. Then turning from Steve to Jennifer, he raised her hand and kissed it with all the affected charm his age and position could command.

"I'm enchanted to meet you, *Señorita* Strand."

What a clown, Steve thought. He'd witnessed this scene countless times before in Lima. A graying middle-aged dandy trying to impress some beautiful woman young enough to be his granddaughter. He probably had a couple of mistresses her age tucked away in Tingo, that is if he'd spent any time at all in this seething cauldron. Jungle girls had a reputation for being great lovers, and easy, so this sleazebag had found a paradise on earth to satisfy all of his lusts. His grandfatherly charm would work wonders. Young, impoverished girls liked the older guys with money. Their sugar daddies took care of them, buying them tacky gifts—like little stuffed animals and silk underwear with flowery lace leg bands—and taking them out to third rate restaurants and to local porn films. The old geezer and his young consort would sit in a dark corner of the theater while she gave him a head job between mouthfuls of popcorn.

"Shall we?" Pierce suggested, gesturing toward a black Ford SUV parked fifty meters away under the shade of a coconut tree. Directly behind it was a military jeep with a soldier leaning against the front fender.

As the group approached the vehicle, the soldier dressed in combat fatigues, and sporting an Galil assault rifle, snapped to attention as he saluted the colonel. Ignoring him, the colonel turned to Pierce and asked, "To the hotel, *Señor* Pierce?"

"Yes, Colonel."

The colonel turned to the soldier and ordered him to follow closely behind.

After stopping to adjust his sunglasses, Pierce stepped around to the driver's side of the vehicle, opened the door, and slid in behind the wheel.

The colonel strutted over to Jennifer, grabbed the back door of the SUV, and gallantly motioned to her to climb in.

Steve had already entered the vehicle from the other side. He couldn't believe how conspicuously daft this guy was. And Jennifer seemed to be impressed by his phony cavalier manner. His graciousness and charm had only one aim, and that was to get into her knickers.

As they roared out of the parking lot, Steve noticed two shirtless teenage boys in ragged shorts watching them, their faces pressed tightly against the thick chain-link fence surrounding the airfield. Their large dark eyes revealed a mixture of fear and contempt as they locked on the SUV pulling out of the parking lot onto the steamy asphalt road.

Sitting next to Steve in the backseat, Jennifer listened politely to the colonel go on and on about jungle cuisine. Then after establishing his reputation as a connoisseur of fine food, he spewed out a host of platitudes about the quaint life in this poverty-stricken third world hell hole. Fortunately, Pierce had turned on the radio, allowing the music to help drown out the colonel's droning voice.

Ten minutes later they entered the outskirts of Tingo María. The SUV pushed its way through the partially paved streets toward the *Plaza de Armas*. Tingo hadn't really changed much, Steve reflected, other than dozens of three-wheeled *mototaxis* clogging the main avenue.

Outside the air-conditioned vehicle, the weather was muggy and oppressively hot, just like he remembered. The sky seemed different though. He recalled mostly azure skies, not the gray, hazy canvass he now saw draped over the town and adding to the overall squalor.

As they slowed behind a slew of *mototaxis* picking up and dropping off passengers, Steve noticed that many of the walls had been painted over with political graffiti from the presidential elections earlier in the year. "Keiko Presidente" stood out among the juvenile gang scribble, the same omnipresent, barely decipherable spray can flourishes one saw on walls and buildings everywhere in Lima, from the poorest to the richest neighborhoods.

The black SUV continued down the busy avenue, gliding silently by a corner tavern. With a mixture of trepidation and loathing, the dark skinned *campesinos* stared at the shiny, expensive vehicle. From the expressions on their faces, the black metallic beast must have looked like a predator ready to pounce on its unsuspecting prey.

The vehicle passed by a store front where two policemen stood in the shade against the front wall, engaged in what appeared to be a light-hearted conversation with two locals. The four of them turned their attention to the tinted windows. They gazed at the dark reflective glass as if it were an omen, the general meaning crystal clear: "We are the rich and powerful and to us your life isn't worth a rat's ass, so you better be real fucking careful."

A few blocks later, the SUV came to an abrupt stop in front of the Esperanza Hotel located on the *Plaza de Armas*. The colonel, the first one to get out of the vehicle, opened the back door and extended his hand graciously to Jennifer.

"Why thank you Colonel Montero," Jennifer said in what sounded to Steve like a mock Southern accent expressing her admiration for his sappy gallantry.

"Juan Luis, to you, *Señorita* Jennifer. I wouldn't want you to think of me as a mere stranger," the colonel replied, smiling expansively underneath his thick, gray-tinted mustache.

"It's good to hear that. I've sometimes had to depend on the kindness of strangers, Juan Luis." She said with a perfect southern lilt as her eyes darted quickly to Steve and then back to the colonel.

"I'll get your stuff, Blanche," Steve said, shaking his head in disbelief. She'd lifted the line right from *Streetcar*. Even if doofus had seen the play, which was doubtful, he was too enamored with her to get the connection. Steve moved around to the back of the SUV, yanked open the rear door, unloaded his camera, his duffel bag, and the two large bags Jennifer had brought along.

"It's been a pleasure, *Señorita*," the colonel replied, kissing Jennifer on her cheek. Then turning his attention to Steve before he climbed into the SUV, "Mr. Collins, I'll send two of my men over in about an hour to transport you to the site of the plane crash. When you get there, ask for Captain Rivera. He's in charge and will be able to answer any questions you may have."

"Thank you," Jennifer said, pulling her baseball cap down on her forehead to block the sun.

"I wish you both safe journey," Pierce said, shaking their hands. "I've already registered your names with the desk clerk. If you need anything, please give me a call." He handed Steve a card from his wallet.

Before Steve could tuck the card in his wallet, Pierce was already into the front seat of the SUV and seconds later shooting off down the avenue.

"Must be in a hurry," Steve remarked as he watched the car sweep around a bus and disappear from sight. Then turning to Jennifer, "Should I ask for a double with a queen size? Or would that upset the colonel? I think the old boy has a crush on you."

"Oh, you, sir, are no gentleman," she said adopting her fake southern accent, this time stealing a line from Scarlet in *Gone with the Wind*.

Steve fired back with, "And you Miss, are no lady."

Rhett Butler's line had her busting at the seams with laughter, especially the way that Steve delivered it. He sounded more like a crass, uneducated hillbilly than a refined southern gentleman.

"No, Rhett, I think I'd prefer a separate room, if that's all right with you. Reuters gives me a handsome per diem."

"Good for you. Polsky complains if I spend more than a few dollars. Okay, partner, separate rooms it will be," he chuckled as they climbed the steps of the hotel and entered the lobby. "We'll pick up our keys at the reception desk and then go off to our 'safe and separate abodes.'"

"Wise decision," Jennifer smiled, apparently enjoying the silly repartee.

She looked so goddamn sexy, he thought, with that Orioles cap pulled down low on her forehead above her lovely dark eyes. And with that knock-me-dead smile.

"What do you say we meet in about forty minutes in the lobby, if that's okay with you, partner." He grabbed the bill of her hat and teasingly gave it a slight downward tug. "I'm going to hop in the shower first. I could use a good back scrub, if you're interested."

"Dream on, buddy boy," she said, shoving her passport across the reception counter to the clerk. "See you in about forty minutes then."

6

Pierce exited the SUV outside his office a few blocks from the hotel. He looked up at the sky, lowering his sunglasses to his nose in order to get a better view.

"Looks like rain, Colonel," Pierce said, speaking through the open window of the SUV.

"We'll probably get the usual afternoon shower. I'll send a jeep over to pick up the two reporters in about an hour. If you need anything, you know how to reach me. Adios."

The sky had darkened and it was as hot and humid as a Turkish bath. Pierce wiped the sweat from his brow. Although the air was stifling, a slight breeze began to stir the air.

Inside his office, the sparse furnishings gave the immediate impression that the place was not open for business. Two empty desks sat in the middle of the room. No pictures on them. No coffee mugs. No folders or papers. Only a thin patina of dust. The waste basket near the front desk had nothing in it. Resting on a table next to the window were a telephone, a computer monitor, a keyboard, and a notepad and pen. Across the room, in the far corner, stood a lonely filing cabinet with a pot of fake, brightly colored flowers on top.

Pierce sat down at the table with the phone, picked up the receiver, dialed, and waited. Light filtered through the cracks in the venetian blinds, casting dark horizontal bars over his solitary figure.

"Hello?" a woman's voice answered at the other end of the phone.

"Is Mr. Henkly in?"

"May I ask who is calling?"

"Tell him it's Frank Pierce."

"One minute, Mr. Pierce, while I see if he's in."

A few moments later Henkly picked up the phone.

"Yes?" he answered, sounding surprised.

"Bill, you didn't tell me a reporter named Steve Collins was coming up here. I thought you were only sending the girl from Reuters."

"I was about to call you, but I've been in meetings most of the morning."

"Look, we have to make sure that Collins doesn't do too much snooping, or things might get out of hand. Whose idea was it to send him?"

"I think Brinton had something to do with it, but why, I'm not sure. As you know, there are certain things I have no control over," Henkly said.

"Looks that way."

"What's that supposed to mean?"

"Forget it."

"I will," Henkly said somewhat piqued. "But I really don't need your off-the-cuff comments."

"And I don't need you to get all bent out of shape either," Pierce said dryly. "If Montero's story plays out, you'll get what you want. And if it doesn't, it's the colonel's baby. He's the one implicating the Shining Path, not you. My object is Montalvo. And I don't want that fucked up."

"Well, we need to work together on this. Just let me know what I can do to help." Henkly said, swallowing his pride.

"I've already taken measures to see that Collins doesn't get too close to the plane, what's left of it that is. The officer that Colonel Montero put in charge of the crash site will take care of Collins. If I have any problems, I'll get right back to you. And if for whatever reason things do not turn out as planned, like always, this conversation, or any other relating to the subject at hand, never took place."

"I understand," Henkly replied, "and do appreciate your help."

7

Jennifer and Steve tossed about in the back of the jeep as it jostled and jolted over a narrow swath of road cutting across the vast jungle landscape. The driver had his eyes glued ahead trying to avoid the deeper ruts while his companion, alert and edgy, kept his Belgian Fal propped at a forty-five-degree angle between his legs. Overhead the sky had cleared and taken on the color of a pair of faded blue jeans.

As the jeep pushed further into the dense brush, the jungle odor became as dank and earthy as a newly dug grave and the road slicker and narrower. The battered, old military vehicle slogged along, the dense jungle scrub scraping its olive drab paint. On each side of the road were trees of every hue of green as well as exotic flowers in full bloom displaying every color of the rainbow. Years ago Steve had spent hours trekking through the Amazon, fascinated by its raw, primeval splendor. He was still able to identify many of the trees, in particular the tall thin *capironas* and trunky *caobas*. Smaller mango trees laden with large pendent fruit and thin, broad-leaf cocoas bursting with cocoa beans hunkered down between the larger trees.

Jennifer turned her head toward Steve and spoke loudly over the whiny gears and the noisy engine. Tiny beads of sweat dotted her brow under the bill of her Orioles cap.

"While I was waiting for you in the lobby, the colonel stopped by the hotel. He explained that he'd come along to the hotel with our military escorts because he needed to give them some last minute instructions."

"I'm sure he did," Steve said incredulously. "And did Juan Luis have roses with him too."

"In a beautiful vase. But if you're not interested, then..."

"No, go on."

"He said the senator's remains would be flown to Lima this afternoon, and that there wasn't much left of the plane because of the explosion and fire."

"There were three other bodies in the plane, right?"

"Correct. The pilot, a Peruvian colonel, and a US Air Force major. The major had gone along to help identify the eradicated coca fields. Sounds like he might have been a horticulturist. The Peruvian colonel was supposedly in charge of giving the senator a tour of the Upper Huallaga, as well as a detailed report on the government's initiative to wipe out coca crops. I don't know if you know this, but Senator Kursten was also the current head of a congressional committee investigating drug trafficking in Latin America."

"Anything on the Shining Path?" Steve asked.

Before Jennifer could answer both of them were tossed a foot in the air when the jeep struck a large bump.

"*Más despacio, por favor!*" Steve yelled at the driver.

"*Si, señor. Lo siento,*" the young driver responded apologetically.

"Yes," Jennifer continued. "He said their intelligence reports show that the decision to shoot down the plane was jointly planned by the Shining Path and the drug lord, Rafael López."

"How convenient."

"What do you mean?"

"Nothing."

"He said that the Shining Path was definitely involved. Two hours after the plane went down, César Montalvo, the Shining Path leader operating to the north of Tingo María, called the headquarters and claimed responsibility."

"And the connection between César Montalvo and Rafael López? What's he have on that?"

"I don't understand," Jennifer replied puzzled.

"He said César Montalvo took credit. So what connects him to López?"

"I didn't ask him," Jennifer answered defensively. "I assume the whole narco-terrorist business."

"Oh, yeah, the *narco*-terrorist conspiracy. The DEA is big on that. It's a hot item again, you know. After all, that's why the US is spending so much money here, somewhere in the neighborhood of thirty-eight million a year."

"That much?"

"Probably more. Ever since the Cold War ended, fighting drugs and global terrorism have been America's new crusade," Steve said, surprised at Jennifer's apparent naiveté.

"So, you're saying the Shining Path doesn't have its hands in the drug business?" she asked, clearly piqued by his condescending tone.

"For sure they're involved in cultivating coca. It's been documented by reliable sources. By that, I mean non-government sources. The rebel leader in this area has formed a committee that works with local farmers to produce coca. The committee is called *Comite Regional del Alto Huallaga*. There's also another Shining Path faction in VRAE, near Ayacucho. This faction appears to be directly involved with the narcos. But it's doubtful that either faction is involved in the drug business for the reasons the State Department gives out."

Jennifer looked away like a school girl who had just been disparaged by her teacher. She apparently wasn't in the mood to listen to his anti-American political rant. He glanced over at her as she stared straight ahead between the shoulders of the two young Peruvian soldiers, refusing to respond to his last comment. She'd puckered her lips into a cute little pout. Not an angry, bitchy pout, more of a sexy school girl pout, which kind of turned him on.

Suddenly the driver swerved to miss a rut, tossing her into Steve. He responded by putting his arm around her. "Hey, I like this. This is much cozier," he laughed.

"You know, you can't be serious for a minute. Sometimes you remind me of a middle-aged teenager trying to impress what he mistakes as his teeny-bopper girlfriend."

It was clear now that she was seriously miffed, but he wasn't sure if it was because of what she saw as his freshness with her or because of his lecture on American foreign policy. In any event, she was making it clear to him that he wasn't going to take her for granted. She had more spunk than he'd imagined.

"I didn't ask for you to come along as my sidekick," she said sharply pulling away from him, her face glowing brighter than ever now, and lovelier.

"Look partner, I think you got it all wrong. I was offered a ride up here on the condition that you could tag along with me. It sounds like Papa Wenton and Uncle Henkly arranged your trip up. Which makes me a little suspicious. You already told me what's in it for *Tio* Henkly. You've pretty much promised him that he could censor whatever you write."

"I think you got it wrong, Stevie boy. I agreed to show him what I write," she said, regaining her composure, and pulling her hat down tighter on her forehead. "That's all. And you know yourself, as a journalist, American Embassy connections are important. If I've agreed to help him, so what? I have the last say in what I publish."

"At Columbia's School of Journalism did they offer classes in buttering up government officials?" Steve fired back sarcastically. He couldn't help himself. He was a wiseass and he knew it. It was just part of his nature.

"I didn't attend Colombia," Jennifer said sharply, truly annoyed now. "I graduated from Brown. With honors," she said haughtily. "And where did you go? Stanford?"

God, she was a little vixen. He relished every minute of it. When she was mad, she turned him on more than JLo's curvaceous ass.

"No, I attended night school at Cleveland State. Within their hallowed halls, we were required to take a class called Ethics in Journalism. I presume, at Brown, you skipped that class," he gibed, really on a roll now.

His last comment caused the annoyed expression on her face to give way to an incipient grin and then a second later to an irrepressible guffaw as she began poking him in the side.

"You're a goddamn smartass, you know! And you really, really know how to piss someone off! That is, until they see through your charade."

Steve realized that it had apparently dawned on her how silly both of them were acting.

"I'll admit to that. I can be a real smartass," he said, totally captivated by the sparkle in her eyes.

"You really didn't attend Cleveland State now, did you?"

"Well, only for a semester or two. Before I transferred to Stanford."

"Yeah, really. Get out of here!" she beamed, her lovely face completely disarming him now.

Another second of looking at this adorable creature beside him and he would be mere putty in her hands.

"Sorry if I got under your skin," he apologized. "I guess I was just trying to impress you and maybe got carried away. I mean what guy wouldn't want to impress someone as cute as you." He gave a quick tug on her hat.

"Well, thank you. I didn't know smartasses could be so sweet," she grinned.

"You know whenever you smile at me, like you're smiling right now, you do a number on my head, girl."

"Okay, let's not get carried away," she said taking his hand in hers. "You know, you're damn funny. Sometimes, that is." And then looking at him with a big PLEASE in her eyes, "But please, let's try to keep things in perspective. We both have a job to do," she implored. "That's what we're up here for, right?"

"Right, partner. Thanks for reminding me," he said reaching into his shirt pocket and taking out a pack of chewing gum. "Want one?"

"Sure."

God, how she drove him nuts. He hoped that his rants the other night and today hadn't given her the wrong impression. At times he must sound like a left-wing fruitcake. He'd really scare her if they moved onto the topic of the environment. A real beef of his. She'd see him as a Green Party freak out to save the whales and whatever else needed saving. Here he was, a forty-one-year-old burnt out journalist, but today she made him feel and behave like a crazy college kid. Goddesses like her could sure do strange things to mere mortals like him.

He was just about to assure her that she had nothing in the world to worry about, that he was as serious about his job as a Catholic priest was about the trinity. But before he could get his first word out, a barrage of machine gun fire exploded from the jungle about ten meters to the left of them. The vehicle swung to the right as bullets struck the driver. He collapsed over the steering wheel while the jeep careened off the road toward a small hill overgrown with thick brush.

The jeep came to an abrupt stop on top of a lump of earth, tossing Steve and Jennifer against the back of the front seats. The vehicle's grill and headlights faced upward at a forty-five-degree angle, the front half of the jeep completely off the ground. Steve immediately grabbed Jennifer by the hand and scrambled over the back of the jeep, pulling her with him. Then half rising, they lunged forward tumbling onto the ground behind a thicket of dense plants.

Steve ended up sprawled out on top of Jennifer. He whispered in her ear not to move and then slid off her. Crouching beside her, he rested his hands on her hips. He raised his head above the plants and looked at the jeep and noticed the two front tires still spinning freely in the air like roulette wheels. As he glanced at the slowly rotating wheels, he wondered if his and Jennifer's chips had been placed on winning or losing numbers. He wasn't feeling optimistic.

A few meters from the front of the vehicle the driver lay motionless. On the passenger side, his companion slumped against the dash, his head wrenched to the side and his face covered in blood. The front windshield, shattered and bloodstained, indicated the spot where his head had struck the glass.

A dozen or so guerillas, dressed like *campesinos,* except for some random articles of military dress—a hat, a jacket, and combat fatigues—emerged from the brush. About half of them wore army boots and the rest makeshift sandals. The rebel who appeared to be the leader motioned to the others to hold their fire. He was a tall, thin man in his late twenties dressed in full combat array. With two rebels flanking him, he moved boldly in the direction of Steve and Jennifer. The soldiers' combats boots made a swooshing sound as they compressed the soft, moist earth.

Jennifer raised herself slowly from the ground. When Steve looked into her terrified eyes, he had an urge to hold her and comfort her, but now wasn't the time. He had to think and think fast. He shot a glance at the dark, impenetrable jungle behind them, and for a second contemplated running for it, but then almost as fast abandoned the idea. Running for it wasn't an option. There were no visible paths, only a mass of trees and hanging vines. The only way anyone could get through that mess would be with a machete.

"Gringos. Come out. Don't be stupid," the rebel leader shouted toward them in English with a heavy Spanish accent.

"Well, if you wanted a firsthand interview, here's your opportunity," Steve said hoping his attempt at humor might put Jennifer at ease. She only returned a half-hearted smile, completely understandable, given their present predicament.

"We have no choice but to cooperate," he said, looking into her panic stricken eyes. "Okay?"

"Okay," she replied nervously, forcing herself to smile, her faced all flushed and her eyes wide with fear.

"We're coming out!" Steve hollered in the direction of the leader. "We're unarmed!"

He took Jennifer's hand and helped her stand.

"Well, kid, here goes," he said.

"Like you said, I don't think we have any other options," she muttered with as much courage as she could muster.

Together they slowly emerged from behind the jeep, their hands held high above their heads.

As soon as they appeared in the open, the leader motioned to several of his men to approach the dead soldier sprawled out near the front of the jeep. They did so and immediately began stripping him, removing everything. His shoes, socks, shirts, pants, any articles they could salvage.

Jennifer shot a glance at the half-naked body of the soldier. She placed her hand over her mouth as though she was going to get sick.

The leader looked at Jennifer and then over at the dead soldier. "He won't need them," he said dryly.

He then motioned to one of the rebels over by the jeep. He had Steve's camera case in his hand. "Pépe, bring me the camera," he commanded in Spanish.

A few seconds later a squat rebel with a very broad chest appeared at his side dangling Steve's camera from his short, stubby fingers.

The leader turned to Steve, "Why the camera?"

"We're journalists," Steve said, not hesitating for a second to declare their profession. The fact they were journalists might just save their asses. "We flew up from Lima yesterday afternoon to report on the plane crash."

"*Si, Trabajo para Reuters,*" Jennifer spurted out in a thick American accent, while nervously rubbing the side of her nose.

"I speak English," he said flatly. "Or did you not notice, *señorita?*"

"I'm sorry. I just thought..."

"Both of you. Come with me," he said, handing Steve his camera.

His manner, though brusque, did not strike Steve as crude and unrefined. The fact that he spoke English meant that he was most likely educated, and this put Steve slightly at ease. The guy could just as easily have been an enraged lunatic in charge of these motley rebels. A twisted, deranged soul not thinking twice about raping Jennifer, shooting both of them in the head, and then leaving them in the brush to rot.

"May I ask where you're taking us?" Jennifer asked, her feathers apparently ruffled because of the way he'd cut her off.

"No, you may not, *señorita,*" he answered sharply, and then turning to his short stocky companion said in Spanish, "Pépe, bring something to blindfold them."

Pépe approached the body of the dead soldier the rebels had dragged from the jeep and already half stripped of his clothes. His bare ass was facing up. Pépe stooped down and rolled him over. One of the rebels had ripped off the soldier's bloody cartridge belt and was fastening it around his waist. He stood next to his comrade who was busy trying on the dead man's boots. The soldier's shirt had been too damaged from the blood and bullet holes to be of any use to the rebels, so they'd left it on him but had removed his pants, boots, and underwear. Pépe, still bent over the body, grabbed hold of the soldier's shirt and ripped it off him. The other soldier, with the broken neck, lay butt naked on the ground about ten meters in front of the jeep. It looked like they'd hit the jackpot with him. Nearly everything he'd been wearing was recyclable.

Pépe returned dangling the bloody shirt in front of him. He ripped it in two and then tied a piece of the shirt around Steve's head over his eyes. The other half he tossed to a comrade who blindfolded Jennifer.

As the rebel tied the blindfold around Jennifer's head, she leaned to the side and he had to steady her. She looked like she was about to pass out. When the rebel finished with the blindfold, the leader grabbed her by the arm and pulled her toward a narrow path that descended to the valley below. Pépe used his rifle to goad Steve along behind her. He tensed each time Pépe pressed the barrel against the small of his back. He was about to protest, but realized it was wiser to keep quiet.

As they floundered down the path, Steve heard rushing water and knew they were approaching a river. It was no small tributary. The sound of the current was too strong. Steve guessed the river to be the Rio Huallaga, a large tributary of the Marañon River. He remembered that the Rio Huallaga began at the slopes of the Andes and then disappeared into the swamps of the Amazon Rainforest.

To keep Steve moving, Pépe gave him a solid push with his gun barrel. Steve's foot caught a root and he lost his footing momentarily. When he tried to regain it, his hands shot out for anything to grab and he latched on to Jennifer's cotton shirt. "Sorry," he said, letting go once he'd righted himself. "My foot caught something."

Jennifer didn't say a word. She was too busy trying to keep her own balance while fanning away mosquitoes that had encircled her face.

When they reached the bottom of the hill, the leader shouted out, "Help them into the boats!" One of the rebels grabbed Steve's arm to keep him from advancing.

Two bare-breasted youths standing on a narrow strip of shore near a sampan took Jennifer by the hand and guided her into the boat. Their baggy combat fatigues—the spoils of war—were way too large for their small, thin frames. Over their shoulders they carried heavy AK-47's.

The leader, Pépe, and another rebel climbed into the boat with Steve and Jennifer while several others dragged two more sampans out of the scrub brush near the shore. In no time, they were adrift on the noisy river.

As the small boats bucked against the current, Steve listened to the steady hum of their motors mixed in with the piercing screech of parrots protesting their alien presence. The lugging of the small engine informed him that the boat was definitely moving upstream. How far up, he had no idea. There were literally hundreds of inlets along the river where they could disappear. For this reason, the jungle was a wonderful refuge for the rebels, and for getting rid of hostages, if that was their plan. This chilling realization threw a dark blanket over any other thoughts. What a godforsaken place to meet your end. The river left no footprints, so the army finding them was about as likely as the rebels putting markers on their graves. Or even burying them. Instantly the two soldiers' bloody, naked bodies flashed through Steve's mind.

Christ, if he was thinking of panicking, what was Jennifer going through at the moment? She had not stirred since they plopped him down beside her. Inside she had to be really rattled. He felt like holding her, but the idea wasn't feasible. Surely the rebel leader would not harm her. Nothing about him struck Steve as brutal or savage. Still, all the terrorist rape stories he'd heard over the years made him shudder.

Steve suddenly felt their boat steer hard to the left, maneuvering past some object in the middle of their path or else heading downstream towards them.

Once the pilot had corrected their path, they continued upstream against the current for what seemed like an eternity. Fearful anticipation of what awaited them at the end of their journey had frozen Steve's internal clock. If the rebels were going to kill them, they would've done so by now and dumped their bodies in the river. Why would they have even taken them to the river? They could've disposed of them along with the soldiers and left their corpses to rot under the tropical sun. A thin ray of optimism stole into Steve's mind like a welcomed guest. He needed to hang on to it and keep his thoughts clear. And not say or do anything stupid. Maybe the leader's plan was to hold them hostages. Like the FARC had done with Ingrid Betancourt. They'd kept her for six long fucking years. Of course, she was a former presidential candidate. By comparison, they were just a couple of stupid journalists lost in the woods. Also, the Shining Path was different from the FARC. The FARC had devolved into a ruthless military organization in cahoots with the drug lords.

This ragged band of rebels looked like they benefitted about as much from the drug lords as American Muslims had from Donald Trump's politics. Of course, the rebels could be far more difficult to deal with than drug lords. They might let their ideals get in the way. Fellows like Trump never had that problem. Dealing with people with crazed ideals, however, generally didn't go smoothly. The thought comforted him like a kidney stone. What happened at the Branch Davidian stronghold in Waco, Texas was a classic example of trying to reason with extremists. Extremists on both sides, that is. Trigger happy ATF on one side and cult lunatics on the other side believing their martyrdom promised them a ticket to heaven.

As Steve saw it, the fact that he and Jennifer were journalists was their real ace in the hole. Journalists didn't take sides, or at least weren't supposed to. Besides, it would not be in their interests for the rebels to harm them. The rebels didn't need more bad press. If they were smart, they'd let them go and call it a day. But then, why the ride up the river?

Steve felt the boat suddenly turn hard to the right as the pilot eased back on the throttle. The engine was no longer lugging under a heavy load. They'd apparently entered a small inlet that broke off from the river and its powerful downstream current. Although the blindfold restricted his vision, through its thin fabric he could perceive everything around him descend into darkness. This deep into the rain forest, underneath a dense canopy of tropical vegetation, sunlight was not welcome. Light did not belong here anymore than civilization did. As he breathed in the same mucid air that his prehistoric progenitors had breathed in, he shivered at the thought of what fate had in store for them. If they had to die, he thought, please have it be some other place, not in this god forsaken land.

After numerous twists and turns along the inlet, the sampan finally came to rest near a muddy bank. Tall *capironas* perched high above them on a red, clay-faced cliff.

"César, *al fin, llegamos*," Pépe said, sighing as he killed the motor and grabbed an oar on the floor of the boat. He pushed the oar into the inlet's shallow bottom and steered the boat into the bank.

"*Bueno*," César replied, and then called out to a rebel who appeared on the precipice above, "José, we have visitors! Send some guys down to give us a hand!"

Before Jennifer and Steve could be helped off the boat, César motioned to Pépe to remove their blindfolds.

As Pépe untied Steve's blindfold, it suddenly dawned on him that the person Pépe had just referred to as César just might be César Montalvo. It made perfect sense that he was Montalvo. How many other Shining Path leaders with the name César would be operating in the Upper Huallaga?

César gestured to Jennifer and Steve to follow Pépe up the bank. Steve noticed that Pépe had jammed the two bloody blindfolds in his back pocket. The fact that Pépe had safeguarded them was a good omen, Steve reflected. The blindfolds were kind of like their return tickets.

As they began their ascent up the slippery slope of the hill, Jennifer grabbed Steve's shirttail, slipping and sliding as both of them minced steps trying to maintain their balance. When they finally reached the summit, several makeshift hamlets came into view. The shabby dwellings were located along the perimeter of a large muddy clearing. A dozen men stood milling around exchanging words with the rebels as they entered the clearing. Two women stopped what they were doing and turned gawking at Jennifer and Steve, wondering what in the world these two gringos were doing with César and his men.

The one woman, pregnant, crouched back down near a fire where she had been frying *bellacos*, a sweet smelling banana—a typical jungle staple. A few feet from her, a young boy no more than fourteen or fifteen sat on his hams meticulously cleaning a rifle near the door of one of the bamboo hamlets. The rifle was several inches taller than the boy.

Christ so young, Steve thought. Barely old enough to lift the weapon to his shoulder. So, the Shining Path was still alive and kicking. Although from the looks of things, hardly kicking. What chance did this ragtag bunch stand against a relatively large Peruvian army financed in part by American dollars? And the funds to arm the rebels? According to the Western press, the narcos financed the guerillas with their drug money. If true, the guerillas needed to form a union and bargain for higher salaries. If the rebels were helping the drug lords move billions of dollars of illicit drugs, they were definitely getting screwed.

César gestured to two skinny soldier boys to give up their seats. They were sitting on wooden fruit crates in front of what appeared to be the general store, or *bodega*. They'd been tossing dried kernels of corn to a scrawny rooster. The rooster pecked mechanically at the dirt, raised its head, shook it, and then craned its neck, looking for the next kernel to be flung in its direction. Hanging over the door of the *bodega* was a Fanta sign, a popular orange drink. And on the *bodega's* thatched wall, attached by a rusty hook, a laminated poster of a Cristal beer advertisement. Steve guessed the poster was there to lend a little verisimilitude to the tiny store, make it look like a real *bodega*. Certainly in this remote refuge—miles from civilization—there was no need to advertise.

Jennifer and Steve took a seat on the wooden crates. César turned to the youngest of the two boys and said, "*Dile a Ana que nos traiga algo de comer.*" The kid hurried off in the direction of three women standing around a large cooking pot suspended from a rusty contraption fabricated out of rebar, half-inch-thick steel rods used in construction.

"Comrade, who are these gringos?" asked a voice in Spanish. The words came from the rebel who'd been standing above on the cliff when they arrived. He had a mustache that curled down over the corner of his lips, which gave him a perpetual frown. He also bore an uncanny resemblance to Che Guevara. His outfit contributed to the impression, in particular the black beret he'd shoved down tightly on his forehead. It looked just like Che's, except without the star. The only other detail missing to complete the image of the martyred iconic leader, was the cigar.

"They say they are journalists," César replied.

"And you believe them, comrade?"

He said this with raw vehemence in his voice. Steve shot a glance at Jennifer sitting on the crate beside him. She looked like she was about to go into cardiac arrest. Judging by the rebel's belligerent attitude, he could be bad news.

"I don't know. What do you suggest we do with them, José?"

"Not sure. About him," José said, nodding to Steve. "But about her, I think I know."

He strolled over to Jennifer and stood above her, his eyes traveling over every inch of her of her body.

"Now this is nice," he said, reaching down and grabbing a strand of her hair and then rubbing it between his thumb and index finger. "Your hair is real soft, *señorita*. Very silky and thick. I like that."

He let go of her hair and stepped around in front of them.

"Journalists, you say. This gringo doesn't look like a journalist. Looks more like a spy, like a CIA pig. The same *malditos* that have a three-million-dollar price on your head."

"Yeah, CIA, you're probably right. What do you think Pépe?"

Pépe looked dumbfounded. He glanced at José. Then not knowing what to say, he looked at Steve and Jennifer, like maybe they would make it simple and tell him whether they were spies.

"Well, let me see if we can find out," José said, stepping away, a diabolical twinkle in his eye. "I'll be right back."

He disappeared around the hut behind Jennifer and Steve, scattering a hen and her peeps.

Steve noticed an odd smirk forming on César's face. Evidently, he'd misjudged him. He seemed to be taking a sadistic delight in the proceedings, like a puma playfully torturing a couple of birds trapped between its claws. Steve had to do something. But what? When this José returned, maybe he could grab the pistol he had strapped at his waist. That's if he moved in close enough to spring up and snatch it. From the look on their faces, these bastards might be capable of anything, and if he didn't do something, and fast, he might not get another chance.

As soon as José returned, Pépe moved in closer to get a better look at what José was planning. Steve glanced at Pépe's chubby fingers squeezed around the trigger of his AK-47. If he went for José, Pépe would turn him and Jennifer both into Swiss cheese. He could feel the arteries in his neck throbbing telling him this could be it.

Jennifer squeezed his hand as José came up to her, positioning himself a few inches away, blocking out the sun and casting a thick shadow over her and Steve. He stood stone still, massaging his knuckles, not saying a word. The area around them grew deathly silent. He suddenly stopped rubbing his knuckles and reached slowly behind his back.

Steve tensed, his eyes fixed on Pépe's trigger fingers. He'd be foolish to make a move, but he couldn't just sit there and let this sadistic bastard have his way with them. Before his thoughts could coalesce into action, José's hand flashed from around his back and went for Jennifer's throat. Steve sprung up off his crate, but César grabbed him from behind and pushed him back down. Lucky for him. The object José held under Jennifer's chin was a long, white chicken feather.

When Pépe saw the look on Steve's face, he roared out laughing. He stopped for a moment and turned to José. "*Compadre*, you really had me fooled. And the gringo too."

José gently placed the feather in Jennifer's hair. "A present for you, *senorita*. As you can see, we're not the mad dogs the *capitalistas* make us out to be," he said grinning.

César released his grip on Steve and ambled over to where Pépe had laid Steve's backpack. He opened it and retrieved Steve's wallet and passport. He nodded to José to join him as he shuffled over towards the *bodega*. Pépe followed right behind, shaking his head and laughing.

Steve turned to Jennifer. "I didn't find their little game all that amusing. That shaggy-haired rascal they call Pépe seemed to get a big bang out of it, though. And you? Are you okay?"

"I guess so. But I'm not sure. All I know is that I was scared out of my pants when I saw his hand go for my throat."

"Yeah, it was hardly amusing."

"So why do you think they brought us here?" Jennifer asked, still slightly dazed. "For fun and games?"

"I wouldn't know. Maybe for lunch," Steve said, removing the feather from her hair and handing it to her.

She studied the feather for a few seconds and then a grin slowly formed on her lips. "Well, it was kind of funny, I have to admit, though I didn't enjoy my part as much as they did."

"Yeah, well, I can understand that," he said squeezing her leg gently. "Hey, you smell the *bellaco*? It has me drooling. My maid is from the jungle. She makes it for me all the time."

"Sounds like a tough life you got back there in Lima."

"You won't hear me complaining."

Jennifer's expression suddenly changed. "I would like to know what plans they have for us."

"I'm not sure if this helps, but I don't think they mean to do us any harm. My guess is that they want something from us. What that is, I don't know. But while we're guests, we should make the best of it. Maybe get their side of what happened to the plane? Assuming, of course, that they know anything about it."

"Their side? Know anything about it? You must be joking. We already know what happened to the plane," Jennifer said sharply, both eyebrows arched, emphasizing her disbelief. Steve noticed the eyebrow thing the other night at his apartment. It was a cute habit she had whenever she wished to show her incredulity.

"Look," he said reaching over and brushing a bug off the bill of her cap, "you know what the American Embassy told you. Nothing more. The truth is the American Embassy folks know only what is convenient for them to know. They're big on pushing their convenient truths."

"What was that you just knocked off my cap?"

"Looked like one of those jungle scorpions, you know the ones that when they sting you, can paralyze you."

"Get out of here," she laughed. "It looked no bigger than an ant."

"Well, it could have been one of those killer ants, you know, the ones that…"

"Can you be serious for a minute?"

"Sure, sorry, what were you saying?"

"I was about to say that I have my doubts that Mr. Steve Collins sitting right next to me on his wooden crate is an authority on terrorism. He writes a feature article in *The Atlantic* a few light years ago and he thinks that makes him a scholar on Latin American politics."

"No, not a scholar. But I probably know a hell of a lot more about the rebels than your brainwashed friends at the American Embassy do."

"Do you now? And you're not brainwashed? I'll just call you Mr. Objective then. I'm sure your reporting has always been right on the money."

"Look, Jennifer, I know Henkly believes the plane was struck by a missile launched by the Shining Path. Maybe it was, but I would rather reserve my judgment until we have the facts. We're journalists, not propagandists. We don't work for the American Embassy, you know."

"Yes, that's right. And I'm not on the US government's payroll. I was just repeating what the colonel told me, not Henkly. The colonel said a missile struck the plane. I wasn't passing judgment or backing anyone's story. Neither should you."

Her argument didn't mollify him. Why should it? She appeared to him to have an obvious bias in favor of the American government and its cohorts. And she needed to see it.

"I'm sure Juan Luis was quick to fill you in with all the important details," he said. "The details the American Embassy wants you to remember." He immediately regretted what he'd said. That was hardly the way to get her to see anything, except that he was acting like a stupid shit.

César, José, and Pépe returned just in time, followed by a girl carrying two plates of *bellacos* and rice. Pépe hunkered down on his hams near Jennifer. César nodded to the girl to serve their guests.

César then said something to José. When he finished, José turned to Jennifer and Steve. He was no longer sporting his beret. It had probably been part of the act.

"It has been a pleasure, gringos, but duty calls. *Buenas tardes.*" He took a step in the direction of the path they had ascended and then stopped. "Yes, and don't forget to write the truth about us," he winked. Then placing an olive drab cap on his head, he turned and headed off.

"Eat. Then we'll take you back to the main road into Tingo María," César said flatly.

"Then we're free to go?" Jennifer asked, astonished.

"Unless you want to stay and join us," he said smiling, his first genuinely warm expression. Then turning to Steve and addressing him in a more serious tone, "We checked the documents in your bag. And since you both appear to be what you say you are, *periodistas*, we have no reason to detain you and wish you no harm. One thing though…" He paused for a few seconds to swallow his food and lick his fingertips before continuing. "You mentioned that you came up here to report on the plane crash. Maybe I can help you."

"Help us?" Steve asked, surprised by César's offer.

"We have information about the plane and what happened to it. There are two…how do you say, *testigos?*"

"Witnesses," Steve said.

"Yes, witnesses, an old man and his grandson. They live close to where the plane crashed. About fifteen kilometers from here."

Steve looked at Jennifer and could imagine her thinking, *Yeah, I'm sure you have a gang of witnesses willing to provide your account.*

"I can tell you what we were told," Steve began, hoping to win the rebel leader's confidence. "Colonel Montero told Jennifer that the plane didn't crash. That it was shot down by a Javelin missile launcher. One of a half a dozen acquired by the Shining Path."

Steve immediately felt like retracting his statement. It had been a mistake to divulge confidential information Jennifer had given him. He looked at Jennifer to get her reaction. Her raised eyebrow told him what he'd guessed. He'd acted incredulously stupid.

"*Colonel Montero! El cabrón!*" César exploded and then spat in the dirt. "*Perdoneme, señorita,*" César said apologizing for his crudity.

Cabrón, was equivalent to saying cocksucker in English. "The man is a liar and a bastard! I learned yesterday morning, not long after the crash, that the plane had fallen from the sky. That the engines were not working. The plane just fell from the sky and crashed."

"Are you César Montalvo?" Jennifer asked out of the blue.

"Yes I am, *señorita*. And everything Colonel Montero said is a lie. The plane was not fired at. It exploded when it hit the ground. We had nothing to do with the plane crashing."

"You say it exploded after hitting the ground?" Steve asked.

"Yes. That is what I was told. I was not there. The old man and the grandson told us what happened. They saw everything. They did not want to go to the authorities. They do not trust them. Many *campesinos* have seen their loved ones disappeared. They are afraid to be disappeared, so they do not speak to the police and military."

"Disappeared?" Jennifer asked.

"Si. Montero will want to..., how do you say in English...*esconder la verdad*. 'Cover up the truth.' And they are afraid. He covers it with a meter of dirt. We are not like those bastards, we do not kill innocent people."

"And the soldiers this morning? Our escorts?" Jennifer studied his face.

"They were dead when they chose to serve the *capitalistas* that hold their brothers in servitude. They are not on my conscience."

"And the US congressman? Wasn't he just another *capitalista*? Wouldn't you have killed him too, if you had known he was on the plane?" She was confident she'd plastered his ass to the wall and he had no wiggle room.

"It would not have been in our best interests, though there are those in your country that would have liked this very much. They would do anything to give a reason for your people to send more money to support this *puta* government."

"The congressman who died was the head of a congressional committee sent here to investigate whether the Peruvian government is really destroying coca fields. Nothing more. He wasn't taking sides," she added.

"Not taking sides!" César spat out. "And your government is not taking sides in Bolivia either. Not taking sides when your *congreso* and your president tell the Bolivian President Evo Morales and the *indigenas* of Bolivia that they have no right to grow what they have grown for centuries!"

"Our government does have a right, if that coca is turned into cocaine and ends up on our streets!" Jennifer shot back.

"Look, to us drugs are poison, and they will have no place in our society. Chewing coca leaves is a tradition, part of our culture. Producing coca for the Mafia drug lords to make cocaine is not."

"Isn't it true that you charge the *narco-trafficantes* for your service?"

"We protect the interests of the *campesinos*. They have the right to plant potatoes, rice, beans, corn, and coca if they choose. Consuming coca is part of their way of life. But they are not the ones making money from coca plants. It's Emilio Martinez and Rafael López, men like them who make money. And this is a problem, especially now."

"Why do you say especially now?" Jennifer looked surprised by his comment.

"Because they have their own army. And they are not *revolucionarios*. They would not have a business if they did not have, how do you say, *conecciones* with the government. We are fighting two enemies—the corrupt Peruvian military and the drug lords. It is a shame that we are shedding our brothers' blood, all because of money and capitalist greed."

"And you are not in the cocaine business?" Jennifer asked.

"Not for long. We need money to operate so we have become involved out of necessity. But not with the *narco trafficantes*. We work with the campesinos directly. But like I said, in the future, there will be no place for drugs. We do what we do out of necessity."

Steve sat listening and watching the exchange between Jennifer and César Montalvo. He had heard most of it before, but not firsthand. In the past, some of the rebels did take money to protect the coca growers, but according to César these new rebels wanted nothing to do with the narcos. How true that was, he wasn't sure. But if true, it could account for the rebels' lack of funds and small numbers. If this underfed scraggly bunch represented an arm of the Shining Path, then the Peruvian government really had little to concern themselves with. From what he could see, the camp consisted of mostly a small band of ragtag, ill-equipped rebels, underfed kids, and tired looking, malnourished women. The camp would be lucky to withstand the onslaught of a strong storm, let alone the Peruvian army.

"Would you pass me your camera please, *Señor* Collins?" César asked, holding his hand out to Steve. He took the camera from

Steve and then gave it to Pépe. Then he motioned to Steve and Jennifer to stand up. When they did, he stepped between them and placed his arms over their shoulders.

"Pépe, please take a photo of the *señoritia*, me, and the *señor*," he said in Spanish. "They can show it to their gringo friends. And to the *son of a whore,* Colonel Montero."

After Pépe snapped off a couple of shots, César told him to give the camera to Steve and, when he and Jennifer were finished with their food, to take them to the main road into Tingo Maria.

8

Steve and Jennifer stood holding onto the rails as the old Ford stake-bed rattled down the half-paved, pock-ridden road toward Tingo María. Leaning against the back of the cab were two field workers in their late forties, dressed in old faded blue jeans and cotton shirts as coarse as their grizzled faces. It was late afternoon and heavy dark clouds pouted overhead stubbornly waiting for mother earth to give the go-ahead. Although a downpour seemed imminent, the clammy air around them had cooled considerably.

The brakes screeched as the old truck came to a stop in the middle of the road and the driver, an old *campesino*, stepped down from the cab and hobbled to the back of the truck. He jimmied the pins free from the tail gate and lifted it off the truck, leaning the gate against the bumper. Waving his straw hat in his hand, he motioned to Jennifer and Steve to step down. His dark, wizened face, baked from the tropical sun, resembled a walnut. As he squinted against the sun, which had momentarily slid from behind a dark cloud, the grooves around his eyes deepened.

"Follow this road about two kilometers until you come to the outskirts of town," he said pointing with his hat.

"*Muchas Gracias, Señor*," Steve replied, reaching in his pocket and taking out a few *soles* and handing them to him. "We appreciate the ride."

As they stepped away from the back of the truck, he and Jennifer waved up to the two *campesinos*. "*Adios!*" Jennifer yelled out.

In concert, the two *campesinos* removed their straw hats and waved back. The driver had already climbed into the cab, and a few seconds later the truck ground into gear and pulled off belching a blue cloud of smoke.

Jennifer raised her arms high above her head and stretched. Then resting her hands on her hips, she shot a weary but relieved glance at Steve. It had been a long day.

"Well, partner, you think we'll make town before sundown?" Steve smiled.

"I don't know. How far do you think Dodge is?" She removed her baseball cap and squeezed it between her legs while fixing her hair into a ponytail.

"When I asked the fellow in the back of the truck, he said about two kilometers."

"So, Cleveland State," she said out of the blue. "And then *The Atlantic*. Quite a leap."

"Well, before the leap, there was a little hopping and skipping in between. I worked for the *Cleveland Plain Dealer* for about two years and got this break when a story I covered made the national news. I'd been doing some investigative work. Mostly on the side. I uncovered a corporate pay-off to a couple of members on the city council. The city's electric company wanted to raise their rates and the pay-off did the trick. I had photos of two city council members meeting in a posh restaurant with a top executive of the company. They'd never dined out before. In fact, there was no evidence that they'd even known each other. And then a couple weeks later both of the council members' bank accounts showed substantial deposits that neither of them could explain to the grand jury. Really stupid on their part."

"So, that got you a job at *The Atlantic*? Just like that?"

"Not exactly. After I applied for a job there, my editor at the *Plain Dealer* went to bat for me. An important friend of his worked for the magazine."

Jennifer picked up a small stone in the road and gave it a toss.

"Hey, pretty good arm there."

"I was a short stop on our softball team in high school. I had wanted to play in college, but didn't make the team. It was probably for the best. I needed to concentrate on my studies to maintain my scholarship."

Steve was about to reply when a thunderous explosion from above stopped him and the wind suddenly gusted, lifting some loose dirt from the road.

"Looks like we're about to take a shower together after all," he laughed. Straightaway the sky had grown two shades darker as a fresh regiment of clouds scudded in from the east. The good news was that about two hundred meters from where they stood in the middle of the road, castellated against the purpling sky, they could make out the jagged roofs of buildings. Steve threw his backpack over his shoulder and turned to Jennifer.

"What do you say we make a break for it? You can show me how quick you are."

"Good idea," she said, and then together they began sprinting towards town. They hadn't traveled more than a hundred meters when huge raindrops began pelting them. They picked up their pace and in a few minutes had reached the outskirts of town. Just as they did, a torrent of rain crashed down, flooding the town and turning the streets into gushing streams. They hurried to get out of the downpour, ducking under an awning of the nearest store.

"Hey that was fun. I feel twenty degrees cooler," Jennifer laughed, breathing deeply, nearly out of breath.

While she stared down at her thoroughly drenched pants, Steve's eyes swooped to the front of her thin rayon shirt soaked completely through, her nipples standing out against the thin fabric.

"Wait here while I get us a taxi," he said.

He dashed out into the cascading rain and flagged down a three-wheeled *mototaxi*. He held the door open as Jennifer scampered from under the awning and into the small compartment behind the motorcycle. She brushed back a long black strand of hair that had come loose from under her baseball cap as she scrunched back against the slick vinyl seat.

Steve crowded in beside her and felt her arm press against his. When he glanced over at her he saw tiny raindrops clinging to the tip of her nose. He thought about how wonderful it would be to lean over and lick them off.

"You need to tell the driver where we're headed," she said, drawing her knees up to her chest and wrapping her arms around them.

"You're right." Steve was suddenly drawn back to reality.

"*Hasta el Hotel Esperanza, por favor,*" he yelled out to the driver above the rain strumming the thin plastic roof.

"Gees, you're as soaked through as I am," she said, smiling that knock out smile of hers and then placing her slender hand on his knee. "Tough day huh?"

"It could have been much worse. It certainly was for our two young soldier escorts. We'll need to tell the colonel about them. And his jeep. No doubt, he'll miss it more than the soldiers," Steve quipped.

"I'll give him a call. God, that was awful. Especially how they just stripped the soldiers down and left them there. Didn't even bury them."

"Not a pretty sight. So, you'll call Montero?"

"Yeah, no problem. What are our plans now?" she asked.

"I was thinking that I would like to follow up on what César said about the two *campesinos* that saw the plane crash. Even though he told us they would never testify. They'd be too afraid of the authorities. Anyway, while we're up here in the Huallaga, we might as well make the best of it and see what we can find out. Maybe there are other witnesses. You up for a little investigative journalism?"

"That's why I'm here. What if we meet later tonight at the hotel bar, say around nineish? Have a drink together," she half whispered in a low, sexy voice. "We could discuss it then."

"I think that's a brilliant idea," he said kissing her lightly on the cheek. "That's for being so damn cool today."

"Well, thanks," she said, and then without warning shot forward in her seat, pointing over the driver's shoulder. "There's our hotel!" she yelled out like some frantic teenager who'd just seen her favorite rock star pass by in front of her. "You need to turn around," she called out to the driver in Spanish in her thick American accent. When she sprung forward, her Orioles cap had brushed the side of Steve's face and ended up on the floor. He bent over, picked it up, and pushed it back on her head, the bill rotated to the back. It looked to Steve like the driver hadn't understood her Spanish.

"There, I like that better. Shows off that cute widow peak of yours. Hey, I guess you noticed, he hasn't turned around."

"Maybe in the rain he didn't hear me."

"*Señor*!" Steve yelled and then pointed toward the hotel. "*El Esperanza! Por ahi!*"

The driver made a quick U-turn that nearly toppled the three-wheeler. Steve and Jennifer just looked at each other, shook their heads and then laughed.

A few moments later the *mototaxi* pulled up against the curb in front of the hotel. Steve paid the driver and then he and Jennifer darted into the hotel lobby. As they entered, a clap of thunder burst forth echoing through the high ceiling of the reception area.

The desk clerk reached over the counter and handed them their keys.

"Phew! *Mama mia*," Steve said while smelling his armpit. "I could use a shower. Are you absolutely sure you don't want to join me?"

"Yes, I'm absolutely 100% sure. You dirty old man," she fired back punching him in the arm lightly.

"I'm not really that old now, am I? Dirty, granted. But old?"

"Well, you're not **THAT** old," she laughed. "Relatively speaking. How old was Methuselah?"

"Who's the wiseass now?"

"Your bad habits are rubbing off. Around nine?"

"I guess that's not too late for this old man," he said, pulling her hat down on her forehead.

"See yah." She marched off toward her room swinging her room key by its chain in a small mesmerizing arc, almost like she was daring him to follow her, or using the room key to work some further hex on him.

9

When Steve woke up, it was nearly nine o'clock. He couldn't believe he'd slept so long, especially with the air conditioning barely working. He threw the sheet back, sprang out of bed, and went over and looked at the thermostat. It was on its lowest setting. He stepped into the bathroom, slid open the glass shower door, and immediately opened the cold water faucet. What he needed was a cold shower to cool him down and remove the patina of sweat he'd collected while sleeping. He dropped his skivvies and eased in under the cold spray. The frigid water jetting from the shower head acted like a hundred icy fingers massaging every inch of his body. One favorable thing he could say about his room. It had decent a shower.

Twenty minutes later he was sitting at the bar working on his second Cuba Libre, waiting for Jennifer and thinking about their encounter with César Montalvo earlier in the day. He couldn't get César's words out of his mind. "We are fighting two enemies, the corrupt Peruvian military and the drug lords. It's a shame that we are shedding our brothers' blood, all because of money and capitalist greed." The news reports claimed that the military was involved in a campaign to destroy cocaine operations in the Huallaga Valley. At least that's what the government had been announcing. So if the Shining Path was working with the narcos against the government, why would César say the rebels were at war with the drug lords?

"Hi handsome." He heard this sweet voice behind him break through his reverie.

He swiveled around on the bar stool and was instantly struck by Jennifer's transformation. She was simply dazzling. Her red satin dress highlighted every lovely curve of her slim figure while its moderately low neckline revealed the top half of her well-formed yet petite breasts. Her hair was combed back and tied off with a cute red bow. With her hair flattened against the side of her face, the high angles of her cheekbones stood out. Steve felt her beautiful dark eyes casting a spell over him again. She was absolutely ravishing. He was speechless.

"Well, what do you think?" she asked, holding out her hand to him. "You like what you see?"

He kissed her hand and then stammered, "You're, ah, just, incredibly…I don't have the word, incredibly… like… like nothing I have ever seen before."

"I'm not sure that's a compliment," she laughed. "I could imagine Beowulf saying the same thing about Grendel's mother."

"No, it was meant to be a compliment. What can I get you?"

"How about a Margarita?"

"Did I ever tell you that you look like a Margarita per…"

"No," she said, cutting him off in mid-sentence. "I'm sure you wouldn't say anything so silly." She settled down on the barstool next to him.

The bar was small and empty, except for the white-jacketed bartender and a couple on the dance floor to the right of the bar. A strobe light above them emitted pulsating flashes of blue light, making their movements look out of sync with the music.

"*Traéle una Margarita, por favor,*" he said to the bartender, unable to take his eyes off Jennifer.

"I never did thank you for pulling me from the jeep," she said, leaning in close to him with her elbows on the bar. Her velvety voice sent goose bumps up and down his arms. "I feel indebted. Thank you."

"That's what partners are for," he winked, raising his glass in a toast.

"By the way I called Montero. He wasn't in, so I explained in my *gringa* Spanish to the officer in charge what happened to the jeep…and the two escorts."

"Your drink, *señorita*." The barman set the Margarita down on the bar in front of Jennifer.

"I still can't believe they left the bodies of those two soldiers out there to rot," she said squeamishly, lifting her drink and taking a sip.

"There's some ugly shit that goes on up here Jennifer. And there's no love between César's bunch and the military."

"Still," she said, twirling the twister stick in her glass. "And the plane? Do you really believe César?"

"I don't know. I've been thinking about it on and off since we left their camp. What would be his motive for lying to us, that is assuming he was behind the senator's death? You said earlier that Montero mentioned he had evidence to link the plane crash to Rafael López and César Montalvo. An unlikely relationship, if you ask me. Especially after César's remark that their future society has no place for drug lords."

"I don't know. Is he being straight? If he is, that would mean Montero might be just using the incident against the Shining Path. I guess it's possible that he's working with the American Embassy to make the plane crash look like something it wasn't."

"That could very well be. Wouldn't be the first time."

"We need to find the old man and the grandson, the ones César said actually witnessed the crash."

"And Montero?" Steve asked. "If César is telling the truth, we'll get nothing from that scumbag."

"You're not jealous are you?" she laughed, remembering Steve's reaction to the colonel coming on to her.

"Hardly. I think he's a little easier to read regarding his intentions toward you, than he is regarding his story about the plane."

"You **are** jealous," Jennifer said coyly, running her fingers through his hair, pushing it back over his ear.

Her fingers in his hair excited him. Was she playing games with him? Reeling him in and out like some poor fish she'd snagged, giving him just enough string to tire himself out before he gave in and she cut him loose and tossed him back into the sea. Well, before the night was over, he was determined to find out.

With his eyes still locked on hers, he rose slowly from his stool, took her hand, and pulled her gently in the direction of the disco lights.

The small space was dark, barely lit, a pulsating blue strobe light the only source of illumination. The song playing was a slow, romantic one, a popular American favorite, "Lady in Red." Steve drew Jennifer close to him and pressed his body against hers.

"Hey, Lady in Red, it looks like your song." He looked into her lovely dark eyes, which now appeared more vulnerable than ever.

"I wouldn't say this is my favorite song, by any stretch of the imagination, but red is one of my favorite dress-up colors."

"Well, you sure look great in it."

Her soft body smelled like a flower garden in the height of spring. As he laid the side of his face against her hair, she snuggled her nose into his neck. He felt the sensual heat of her breath against his skin and thought that he could hold her like that forever.

The song came to an end, but they waited a few seconds before they separated. The flickering strobe light caught the tender features of Jennifer's face as her inviting eyes stared up into his.

"Shall I order a couple of drinks to take to my room?" Steve said, instinctively feeling it was now or never.

"Okay," she said in this somnambulant voice, sounding as though she had not yet awakened fully to whatever it was the night promised.

The young barman, wiping some glasses, glanced over at them and smiled. "Anything else *señores*?"

"Si, two drinks to go. The same, please," Steve said.

The bartender turned to the shelf mirror behind him displaying an array of liquor. While he removed a bottle of José Cuervo and Bacardi from the bottom row, he caught a glimpse in the mirror of Steve and Jennifer kissing. He smiled and then added an extra shot to each drink.

Steve opened the door to his room and switched on the light as Jennifer, lightheaded from the Margarita, held on to his elbow, trying to maintain her balance in her high heels.

"One second," she said, and then gave a kick and watched her shoes sail across the floor and strike a small lamp on the table next to the bed, sending the lamp crashing to the floor. "Wow, sorry" she giggled. "Hope I didn't break anything." She raised her glass, polishing off a third of her Margarita. Then she handed Steve the glass and teetered across the slick parquet floor in her bare feet toward the dresser. As she reached for the dresser top, her foot slid and she almost fell but caught hold of the back of a chair and steadied herself.

"Damn panty hose," she laughed, and then reached under her skirt and pulled them down and tossed them into the corner.

Steve took a healthy swig from his drink and then moved toward Jennifer, setting both of their drinks on the dresser.

She wiggled her finger at the light switch near the door, and Steve complied right away, stepping over and switching off the overhead light.

The streetlight entering through the slit in the curtain rendered the objects in the room only dimly visible, imbuing them with a stark transience that suggested to Steve the finite nature of the moment. She had been leaning back resting her bottom against the edge of the dresser, and when he returned, she reached out and grabbed his belt buckle and drew him closer to her.

His eyes traveled down to her cleavage graciously displayed by the low cut neckline of her dress and then moved up again to her face. He took his eyes off hers only long enough to snatch his drink from the dresser and finish it off. Then setting the glass back down, he reached around behind her and slowly unbuttoned the back of her dress. As he slipped his hands inside the cool satiny fabric, he felt her body quiver slightly. He unsnapped her bra strap. Liberated from their cruel harness, her breasts gave way to gravity and dropped slightly.

She raised her arms high in the air while he slipped the loose dress over her head. At the same moment, her bra fell free and struck the cool parquet beneath them. Naked to the waist, she stood before him, while the faint light from the streetlight outside the window entered through the slit in the curtain, bathing her body in a silvery light. He bent down and began kissing her breasts, his lips eventually traveling upward from her nipples to the heat of her neck. She closed her eyes, relishing his soft, tender kisses against her skin, her head bent back in ecstasy and her long dark hair falling against her pale white shoulders.

10

A mangy gray alley cat scratched at the window. When it failed to attract Jennifer or Steve's attention, it stretched lazily and arched its back. For a full minute it sat on the outer window ledge and waited before it returned to scratching and rubbing its side against the glass. Its persistent scratching eventually woke Steve, who rolled over in bed and shot a glance at the window. When he saw the silhouette of the cat behind the thin curtain, he relaxed and then smiled

The sun barely up at this hour, veiled the room in a thin gray light. Jennifer lying on her side curled up next to him, rested her head halfway on her pillow, her long dark hair spread out in tangles. The sheet pulled down around her waist, left the upper half of her naked body exposed.

Steve quietly raised himself from the bed and tip-toed into the bathroom, careful not to awake her. He turned on the faucet and took his toothbrush out of the water glass resting on the countertop and squeezed a thin bead of paste onto the bristles. As he brushed his teeth, he turned his head and looked through the opening of the door to where she lay on the bed. She had not moved, apparently exhausted from their late night frolicking.

Last night, he had this odd feeling as he cuddled up next to her, her arms wrapped around him, and his head on her breasts. As he lay in her arms, he had this Freudian reflection and wasn't sure what to make of it.

When he was still a young boy—shortly after his father had left them—his mother moved in with a carpenter named Dean who earned his money making kitchen cabinets. Dean also had this passion for building large boats, and had undertaken building one behind their two-story apartment. Why Dean would choose such an expensive project, when he was barely making a living as a cabinetmaker, was anyone's guess. The nearest lake was fifty miles away, so the boat would've been of little practical value to him. Dean never finished the boat, and the only memory Steve had of it was of its skeleton docked in the parking lot behind their apartment on high wooden supports, perched there like a rough draft of Noah's ark. He often wondered in later years what some of Dean's poorer working class neighbors thought of his project. Maybe they saw it as a potential haven, their Doomsday ticket to safety, if the rains got much heavier.

One night his mother unexpectedly became his Freudian ark. It all started when she and Dean entered into a fierce argument. His mother began shouting at the carpenter for foolishly spending so much money on the boat. He remembered Dean storming out of the apartment and leaving his mother sitting in her night gown on the edge of the bed crying. He wasn't sure what to do. He was just a snot-nosed kid and it was the first time he'd seen his mother in tears.

He felt like going to her, but he held back. The truth was, they weren't that close. He was only about six when his father split, and right after his parent's divorce, he ended up spending a couple of years in the care of his Aunt Mary, a sour middle-aged woman, overly religious and strict as hell. Her favorite pastime was kneeling by her bed in the early morning and late evening reciting the twenty mysteries of the rosary.

His aunt was the good Catholic, his mother the loose cannon. Within a few months after his father walked out on them, his mother decided to take off for the west with Dean the carpenter. She told her sister that she would either send for him in a few months or return and pick him up. She had a job promised to her in California. A Jewish friend had opened a furniture store in LA and needed a topnotch saleswoman. And that she was. She had no problem selling Aunt Mary on taking care of her six-year-old nephew while she skipped out for California with Dean. His aunt, and his Uncle Mike, a taciturn autoworker, already had their own son to take care of, but they surmised that since Little Stevie was family, and they were good Catholics, they had an obligation to watch after him.

The few months turned into two years. A year after leaving him, his mother called from California and hinted to her sister that maybe it would be a good idea to put him in an orphanage for a while until she could get her life together. Things hadn't turned out like she thought they would with her new job, and Dean was hardly making ends meet.

His aunt would have nothing to do with the idea of an orphanage for her nephew. The idea of sending him to a home was not at all Catholic. If she abandoned him, she would not be able to live with herself.

As it happened, a good-paying job for his mother, or for Dean, never materialized. After two years on the West Coast, and a half dozen short letters to his aunt, she returned to Ohio and promised this time she was going to stay. Dean stayed behind in

California and threatened to leave her for good, but then relented and joined her a month later.

It would be an understatement to say that he and his mother were not very close. She had rarely showed any real affection toward him. Maybe he reminded her of his father. But that he would never know.

Last night, lying next to Jennifer, he started thinking of that night so many years ago when he was only six. The night Dean rushed out of the house drunk and furious while his mother sat on the bed crying.

And her inexplicable behavior, once the sobbing stopped.

When she'd finished crying, she rose from the bed, went into the bathroom, and came out stark naked. He sat in the middle of the living room floor playing with his toy truck, not knowing what to think. He'd never seen a naked woman before. His aunt, who in her youth had nearly taken her vows as a nun, was not the kind of women to prance around the house revealing any flesh.

His mother went over to him, took him by the hand, led him into the bedroom, and pulled back the bed sheet. Then she slipped under the covers and motioned to him to join her. She reached over and turned off the light on the night stand and in the darkness stretched her arms out searching for his small hands. When she found them, she held them in hers, and not uttering a word, cuddled up next to him and fell asleep.

He snuggled in closer to her, feeling the softness and warmth of her body, listening to her steady breathing and smelling her womanliness mingled with the sweet fragrance of her hair. That night lying there with her, an emptiness that he'd been carrying inside was suddenly filled with the security and comfort of maternal love.

Until last night, he never imagined finding that feeling again. And especially not with someone like Jennifer. She was hardly a mother figure. But then why did last night make him think of that distant childhood experience with his mother?

He rinsed the toothbrush under the running water, closed the faucet, and set the brush back in the glass.

He walked over to the bed and carefully pulled the sheet over Jennifer's shoulders trying not to wake her. For a few moments, he stood there watching her sleep. His heart filled with joy as he thought about how whole and complete he felt last night lying next to her. Like that child so many years ago.

He stepped lightly over to a small table in the corner of the room and picked up the phone to dial room service for breakfast.

As he held the receiver in his hand waiting for the reception desk to answer, a loud explosion suddenly ripped through the air rattling the window glass. The cat, terrified, bolted from the sill. Jennifer sprang up in the bed, her eyes wide open. She clutched Steve's arm. "Jesus! What was that!" she cried out.

"Sounded like a *cochebomba*."

"A what?"

"A car bomb," he replied, quickly pulling on his pants.

He rushed over to the window and pushed the curtain open just in time to see a jeep loaded with soldiers roar by the front of the hotel in the direction of the blast. On the far side of the park, he could make out a thin column of smoke rising above a building.

"I'm going to go see what happened. Stay here for a few minutes until things settle down."

"Okay. Be careful," she said, a mixture of fear and concern showing in her eyes.

Steve slipped on his shoes, pulled on his shirt, and rushed toward the door. He hurried out, slamming it behind him.

"Your camera!" Jennifer yelled after him.

He swung the door back open and hurried in and rummaged through his backpack.

"Thanks," he said as he hurried toward the door holding the camera against his stomach while fidgeting with the settings.

Three blocks away from the hotel in front of the police headquarters, he saw the twisted, smoldering front frame section of a car with only the engine block remaining. Nothing else was left of the car, except part of the bumper and jagged pieces of metal scattered up and down the street. Many of the stores along the street had their windows blown out and one of the shops had its door ripped completely off. Glass, metal, stones, and wood littered the sidewalk and street. Soldiers, police, and onlookers gathered, staring in amazement at the smoldering wreckage and speculating on how powerful the blast had been.

Steve approached the officer who seemed to be in charge, showed him his journalist card, and then began snapping off photos. A jeep squealed to a stop across the street in front of the police station and Steve saw Colonel Montero climb out. The colonel strutted over to the officer in charge, conversed with him for a few minutes, circled the smoldering frame section, and then walked over in Steve's direction.

"*Buenos Dias.*"

"*Buenos Dias,*" Steve returned, while continuing to take photos of the wreckage. "The car must've been jammed full of explosives."

"Yes, it looks like it," the colonel said. "By the way, the officer that *Señorita* Strand called yesterday told me what happened. You two were very lucky. Yesterday afternoon *campesinos* from Machipa, a small village not far from where you were attacked, were murdered."

"Murdered?" Steve stopped snapping off photos and turned to the colonel. "What happened?"

"A dozen or so *terruchos* went into Machipa, took the villagers, many just women and children, said they were *soplones*...how do you say in English?"

"Informers."

"Yes, informers. Took them outside of town, lined them up by the side of the road, and shot them in the back of the head. After they made them dig their own graves."

"When did you learn about this?"

"Yesterday afternoon."

"Were there any witnesses?"

"Not a single one."

"How do you know it was Shining Path?"

"It was obvious. They painted on a wall fifty meters from where the *campesinos* were murdered, *'Esto es lo que le pasa a los traidores.'*"

"This is what happens to traitors," Steve translated.

"Yes, that's correct."

"Still, that's not hard proof that they were *Senderistas.*"

"*Well, Señor* Collins, I don't know what else you..." The colonel suddenly stopped in mid-sentence when he saw Jennifer crossing the street.

She arrived looking pale. The muscles in her face were all tense. While waiting for things to calm down outside, she'd changed into jeans and a light blue blouse. As she approached them, Montero's face relaxed, losing some of its pomp, as he prepared to turn on the old charm.

"*Buenos Dias, Señorita* Jennifer," he sang out as he leaned forward and kissed her on the cheek. "Hope you slept well. Sorry that it's started out as such a terrible morning, as you can see. I know that yesterday was a tough day for you as well. I was telling

Mr. Collins that you were quite lucky. Dozens of *campesinos* were murdered close to where you were."

"Dozens? Close to us? By who?" She looked shocked.

"The Shining Path, *señorita*. They executed forty-three villagers. My men have taken photos of the victims and where they found them. If you think you could use any of the photos, please let me know. The world needs to see what these *terroristas* are capable of, *señorita*."

Just then a young officer hurried over and saluted Montero.

"Colonel. *Tenemos uno de los sospechosos.*"

"Did he say they have one of the suspects?" Jennifer asked Montero.

"Yes, *señorita*."

"Perhaps we could interview him?"

Montero studied her for a second and then said, "Okay, *señorita*. I will make him available to you. One thing though. I don't think that it is safe for you or Mr. Collins to visit the site of the plane crash. There is too much terrorist activity in the area. And your government is involved now. Your embassy notified me that they did not want anyone near the plane."

Then addressing the young officer, he changed to Spanish, "Where is the detainee now?"

"He has been taken to the police station, Colonel."

"Tell the police officer in charge I'll be there soon."

"*Sí*, Colonel."

He turned back to Jennifer. "It's not customary to allow journalists to have interviews with suspects. But, I will make an exception for you, *señorita*," he said, putting on a magnanimous smile. "First we'll need to question him. When we're finished, I'll contact you at your hotel."

"Thank you, Colonel."

"My pleasure, *señorita*."

Then shifting his attention to Steve, "You will need to make a report at the police office about what occurred yesterday. They will need a statement."

"Yes, we'll do that later this morning."

"I understand that the rebels opened fire on the jeep killing the two soldiers. Where were you at the time?"

"The jeep nearly tipped over, allowing us to escape. We hid in the brush nearby."

"Did they fire on you also?"

"No, not really. They asked us to show ourselves. Once we did, they asked us a few questions and went through our stuff. When they found out we were journalists, they let us go."

"Did they identify themselves?"

"No."

"And they simply let you go?"

"Like I said, they looked at our documents, saw we were journalists, and let us go. They took the dead soldiers' weapons, and their clothes, and rummaged through the jeep for things they could use. Then the guy that looked like the leader told us that their war was not with us, or even with America, and that we were free to go."

"Did you get his name?"

"No."

Steve could tell by the way the colonel was staring him down that he didn't believe a word of his story.

"How many of them were there?"

"About a dozen."

"And how did you get back?"

"We stopped a farm truck and hitched a ride."

"Well, you were both very lucky, *amigo*."

"I would like to take a look at the crash site. I know you think it's unsafe, but I can take care of myself. I'd like to interview any *campesinos* that might have been nearby when the plane went down."

Steve waited a moment to see the colonel's reaction and then continued. "After all, that's why I'm up here, Colonel, to cover the crash."

"Mr. Collins, like I said, I was notified yesterday evening that the American Embassy has taken over the investigation. I have orders that no one is to be allowed near the crash. I asked if that included you also. I was told it did. The whole area is off limits."

"Okay," Steve said, "but I do plan to interview anyone in the area who might have seen the plane crash."

"No one saw anything," he replied angrily, raising his voice an octave. "No one was around when the plane was shot down, except the Shining Path. I had my men personally interview everyone within twenty kilometers of the crash. No one saw anything. So there is no one to interview. Except me."

The colonel paused, his eyes drilling into Steve's. "You had an opportunity yesterday to ask the terrorists. Why didn't you?

They've already claimed responsibility for shooting down the plane. So, what more do you want?"

"Colonel, it wasn't exactly the right time to conduct an interview. We were happy to get out of there alive, especially after what happened to the two soldiers."

A few tense moments passed while Montero's eyes remained trained on Steve. It was clear that he did not trust Steve, or believe the rebels simply let them go without having a conversation about the plane.

"Mr. Collins, I don't want to be responsible for your death. So you will stay away from the area surrounding the crash site. That directive is also coming from your embassy."

"We appreciate your concern Colonel. And our embassy's," Steve replied dryly.

Jennifer had not said a word. She stood to the side listening. The colonel must have noticed that she'd become uncomfortable. Deliberately changing the subject, he turned to her and said, though with little real conviction in his voice, "I'd like to say that I'm sorry about what happened to the American senator. I forget to mention that yesterday. You have my condolences, *señorita*."

"Thank you, Colonel."

"When I'm done with the detainee, I'll call you at the hotel and let you know when it's okay to go to the police station and conduct your interview. Take as long as you think is necessary. If you need anything at all, any help with the interview, please let me know. I would be more than pleased to assist you." He leaned forward and they exchanged kisses on the cheek. Then he turned to Steve and said flatly, "*Buenos Dias,* Mr. Collins."

Once he was out of sight, Steve said to Jennifer, "Can you believe that asshole? How he was coming on to you? I guess I'll need to get permission from you to interview the detainee, since Juan Luis made it a point to exclude me."

"Yeah, well, we know he's a dick, Steve." She wasn't smiling now. Steve had his back to the sun, so she had to squint while looking at his figure framed in the bright light. She raised her hand against her forehead to shield her eyes from the sun.

"But, Steve, I'm not sure what you were up to. It looked like you were trying to piss him off, give him a reason not to like you, and not to cooperate. We need to find the two *campesinos* César mentioned. We don't want the colonel getting in our way. And if you piss him off, he'll be in our way big time."

Steve knew she was right. His head dropped like some poor dog's scolded by its master for pissing on the floor. Her words had pricked him to the marrow. His obvious contempt for the colonel certainly hadn't made things easier.

"I'm pleased that you didn't mention César to him, or our visit to his camp. That was smart," she said, apparently feeling sorry for being a little hard on him.

"Thanks. Look, I wasn't trying to piss him off. I don't trust him, that's all. Either he's lying or César's lying. Why should I trust him more than César? They both have their agendas."

"I agree, so we're better off not sharing information with the colonel, until we know more. And not rattling his chain. Okay?" she pleaded, using her disarming smile.

"Sure. I'll do my best." Steve raised his camera and snapped off a photo of a soldier standing near the smoldering car frame while a boy about nine was stooping over collecting a piece of metal from the explosion.

"He'll probably keep the metal as a souvenir."

"How grisly," she said.

"Yep."

"Hey, let's get breakfast when you're done taking photos. In the meantime, I'll see if any of the folks around here saw anything before the blast. Then we'll see if we can rustle up some pancakes and coffee, partner."

"Sounds like a good idea. But you ain't gonna find no pancakes around here."

"Then I'll settle for hot coffee and toast with jam."

"Coffee and toast it is. I'll buy. Where's your Orioles cap?" he asked, running his hand over her ponytail. "I miss that tomboy looks it gives you."

"You didn't seem to miss the tomboy look last night. I wasn't exactly dressed like a tomboy then."

"As I recall, you weren't dressed at all."

"Your lucky night."

"Think the stars will line up for me again?"

"That I wouldn't know. You know how fickle fortune is."

"Yeah, about as fickle as a woman's heart."

"Whoa! What do we have a poet here? A bit sappy though, don't you think?"

"Yeah, a little. Give me another five minutes and then we'll get that coffee."

11

Ambassador Wenton was sitting at his desk reviewing reports when he saw the red light on his intercom begin flashing. He reached across his desk and pressed the button.

"Yes, Ms. Clark?"

"Mr. Ambassador, John Brinton is here to see you."

"Send him in please."

As soon as Brinton walked through the door, Ambassador Wenton could tell from his friend's tense expression that he wasn't going to be the harbinger of good news.

"Good afternoon, Frank."

"Good afternoon, Ambassador. Bill Henkly just sent my office this god awful list of emergency military support requests from the minister of the interior's office. They're asking for an immediate assistance package of about fifty million dollars! Can you believe that? Talking about escalating matters."

"Thank God the Secretary of State's office isn't likely to move quickly. In the past, they've been reluctant to give the green light to any sort of direct military intervention. I doubt that we'll see any presidential support for escalating matters here, though most of the damn newspapers and TV reports have already connected the congressman's death to the Shining Path and Rafael López."

"I agree, but once Fox News begins its propaganda campaign to paint the president as spineless, and the congressional hawks begin circling him, making demands and threatening to block any bills he would like to see passed, who knows what might happen. Politics in Washington is always full of surprises."

"Do you have a list of the items the Peruvian military is requesting?"

"Yes," Brinton said, flipping through some papers he had brought with him. "It's pretty complete."

The ambassador noticed the intercom's red light flashing again. He bent over his desk and pressed the button.

"Yes, Ms. Clark?"

"Mr. Ambassador. Bill Henkly's here. He says it's urgent."

"Okay, send him in." Then to Brinton, "For Christ's sake. What does he need now?"

Henkly entered the office looking grave. "Good morning, Mr. Ambassador. Carl Singler informed me late yesterday that the Shining Path staged a purging of a small village near Tingo María, murdering forty-three *campesinos*, many of them women and children."

"A purging? Over what?"

"It seems the village of Machipa had been passing information about Shining Path members to the army. Well, the Shining Path decided to 'teach' the village a lesson. Though God knows it's a horrible thing to say, the killings might have come at the right time. This might be what it takes to get the full congressional support we need. The Peruvian military is in desperate need of combat supplies and equipment. Without helicopters, surveillance planes, jeeps, weapons, in short, serious committed US backing, we will be fighting a losing campaign against narco-terrorism. This place will turn into something worse than the drug war in Mexico. At least Mexico's not threatened by an insurgency."

"An insurgency? Let's not blow things out of proportion. I was just discussing the report for military emergency support you sent to John's office. Please send me a complete copy of Mr. Singler's report on the Machipa incident."

"I'll have it to you this afternoon, Mr. Ambassador. Anything else?"

"No, nothing right now, thank you."

As Henkly departed, Wenton imagined how delighted the son of a bitch must be. He looked at Brinton and knew he was thinking the same. Henkly had to be salivating at the thought of US military involvement. The Machipa killings could pour gasoline on a brush fire that looked ready to flame out of control. Brutal massacres were a common occurrence in the late 80s and early 90s, but nothing like this had happened in more than twenty years. And according to Henkly, many of the victims were women and children. At least that's the information he received from Singler. How terrible. The thought of such heartless and senseless violence revolted him.

No doubt the terrorists and the narcos had to be dealt with. That was a given. But was sending more money for weapons the solution? That's what bothered him about characters like Henkly and Singler. They couldn't think outside of their olive drab box. For them, the military always held the answer. First support the Peruvian military, and if they couldn't do the job, send our guys in. Begin with covert operations. Bring in the Singlers. And if any of the politicians on the left back home get too noisy about intervention, use the drug war as an excuse for more money and then funnel it to the CIA. David Kursten had been right. Little of the US aid to Peru was used to directly fight the drug war. The target wasn't the drug lords. The target was the Shining Path. But forty-three dead *campesinos*. The Shining Path claimed they were fighting for the poor, the exploited. Fighting for the victims of political corruption and a heartless economic system. How could that be when they murdered poor *campesinos* and worked together with the drug mafia in order to finance their revolution?

"Well, John, if this bloody business continues, it looks like the Peruvian military is going to get what they asked for," Wenton said, ending his reverie.

Brinton had been standing quietly staring out the window into the gray diaphanous afternoon.

"Sometimes, Frank, I think we chose the wrong careers," Brinton sighed.

"You won't get an argument from me on that point," Wenton said flatly. "I sure in hell felt more at home around my academic colleagues than I do around the likes of folks like Henkly and Singler."

"I have to confess that lately I've been feeling it's about time to give it a rest, Frank. Maybe return to teaching. That's the one side of me talking. The other side tells me we have a higher purpose right here. I just hope those *campesino* murders are not an example of history repeating itself."

"Let's pray it doesn't, John. Peru lost over 70,000 in its war on terrorism. Although Singler and Henkly's zeal is troubling, it's not in anyone's best interests to stand back and let the terrorists have their way. Not in Peru's best interest, for sure, nor in ours. Whether or not we relish our role, it's a big one, and we must do our best to fulfill it."

12

Around noon Jennifer received a call from Colonel Montero. He informed her she could conduct the interview with the detainee anytime in the afternoon. Steve thought they should go to the police station first and file their report about the incident yesterday with the rebels.

They waited in a cluttered room while a paunchy, graying middle-aged cop sat at a small desk with an old Hewett Packard in front of him working on their report, one finger on each hand pecking at the keyboard like the beaks of two barnyard hens bobbing for seeds. The police station, a large brick two story suburban dwelling, had been acquired in a drug raid. No prisoners were kept there. Steve and Jennifer sat in metal fold-up chairs in what was once the living room, crowded now with filing cabinets, gray metal desks, three old computers, a tired, worn out printer, and boxes of archived reports stacked against the walls.

Twenty minutes into the report, the lights flickered in the building and the power went off. Then a second later the power miraculously returned. The officer sat dumbfounded looking at a blank screen, wondering where his report had vanished. He apparently had no concept of cyberspace and how digital information could disappear into a black hole never to be seen again, unless of course the 0 and 1's had been recorded on the machine's hard drive. That entailed pressing the save keys at reasonable intervals as he typed. Another concept foreign to him.

After Steve and Jennifer sat suffering through more than an hour of the officer retyping the report, it was finally finished and their tortured souls were free to go.

When they returned to the hotel, they agreed to meet in the lobby around five and then walk over to the police station together for the interview. Jennifer said she needed to shower and take a short nap. Steve decided to get a beer.

He walked across the street to the corner store, bought a couple of cold Cristals, and returned to his room. Once inside, he turned the air up full blast and kicked off his shoes. The hotel had promised to repair the air conditioning unit and it seemed to be working fine. For how long was anybody's guess. He popped the cap off a beer using an opener attached to the min-fridge and then stretched out on the bed, his head propped up on the pillow.

Moments before, out in the hotel lobby, he was getting these bad vibes from Jennifer. He couldn't put his finger on it. He sensed that she might be thinking it would be better to cool things down a little. During breakfast she kept going on about how strong the margaritas had been. That back home they were watered down versions of those last night. She made it a point to mention she had trouble walking straight after the first one. The more she prattled, the more it seemed she was searching for an excuse to explain away the beautiful thing that had happened between them.

The mind of a woman, not an easy thing to figure out, he reflected. He really had no idea what she was thinking. It was all speculation. And it wasn't like he could be objective about her either, so he needed to step lightly when it came to drawing conclusions about her feelings toward him. All he knew for certain was that never before had he been so charmed by a woman.

Not only was she adorable. She felt right for him. Compatible. Except, maybe her politics. But that was okay. No doubt about it, her beauty was definitely part of the attraction. He'd be a damn liar to deny it. He'd known many pretty women, had developed into somewhat of a lady's man even, no small thanks to hanging out with his buddy Gerardo. He'd certainly had his fair share of young gorgeous ladies. Not that he was proud of his conquests, if that's what they were. In Lima it was easy for a gringo to pick up pretty women, and as a result his life had become full of short, stupid romances that lasted no longer than a bottle of Bacardi.

But Jennifer was the real thing. He felt connected to her both physically and spiritually. Although he hated using the word spiritual to define relations between the sexes, he just couldn't think of better word. He could say intellectually, but that wasn't it either, though the fact that she was smart had to be part of the connection. She was clever and tuned in. That's how he'd describe her. And she actually enjoyed his wry sense of humor, which most Peruvian women didn't get or didn't think funny.

Years ago, in his college days, there was this girl named Julie. They had something special too. She was fun to be around, cute, droll, and sexy. With a biting wit. And a lovely, freckled face. Usually he didn't find freckled faces all that attractive, but her freckles fit her face perfectly, kind of like the splashes of black fit a Dalmatian. If you removed them, a good part of the beauty was lost. She also had these beautiful hazel eyes and this silky, reddish brown hair that fell just to the nape of her lovely thin neck. And, yes, this seductive lisp that drove him bonkers!

Not everything about her was feminine. She had a tomboy quality about her that turned him on, though this was a harder thing for him to understand. Their love making would usually begin with her teasing him and poking him playfully. Then she'd begin rough housing, until her provocations ended in a silly wrestling match, which he began to see as a rough kind of foreplay.

Her pleasing face was nothing in comparison to her body. It was a body that could launch a thousand ships, or better yet a thousand erections. If Helen of Troy had her body, her face would have been superfluous in getting those Greek and Persian boys all fired up. After all these years, Julie's body was a gift that his mind still treasured. He would always remember those shapely breasts, how they curved upwards like an offering to the gods. And grand theft for mere mortals. And her ass, it could make an hour glass blush in shame at being out curved.

Nights with her in bed were a virtual marathon of love making that left them both utterly exhausted. The next day they had to summon all the energy they had left in their limp young bodies to lift themselves from their love making nest and descend into the real world of nine o'clock classes.

She was a psych major and loved to engage him in conversations about Freud and fixations, Jung and the Collective Unconscious. She was always in the habit of psychoanalyzing him, though with no concrete results. She concluded he was potty trained too early and that's why he never liked to leave large tips and never gave himself completely to her, emotionally that is. He never did get the connection between tips and his emotions. Freudian claptrap never did much for him anyway.

She seemed to project pure energy, physical and mental, and that's where she and Jennifer were alike. But when it came to what he understood about true love and finding your "soul mate," if there was such a thing, there the comparison ended. What he felt for Jennifer last night when he lay next to her after they had made love belonged to a different class of love, a rare thing he had only imagined and never experienced—that is as an adult. It was a love that needed nothing to convince him of its veracity. Nor did it judge him. It was a warm, naked, silent, secure love, the kind that he wanted to believe never broke promises. A love that would never desert him. Nor reject him. The kind of love he had always longed for but had never found.

What he and his freckled goddess had had between them wasn't like that. It fizzled out over their junior year. He wasn't sure who lost interest in whom first, but the relation began to cool during the beginning of the second semester and arctic winds moved in before the semester ended. For weeks, they had secretly grown bored with each other and had upped the stakes to see if the relationship would last. More sex and exaggerated passion. As expected, the ante was too high. Their love making wasn't enough to keep the fires alive and drive out the chill, so the kindling sparks, barely aglow, soon faded to lifeless gray ashes.

A month after they split she was hotly in love with this nerdy biology major that she met at a dorm party. And Steve was history, but free. Whenever he saw her, she wouldn't give him the time of day. They'd exchange a quick hello when they passed each other on campus, and then she'd hurry off, saying she was late for class, or some such rot.

"Frailty, thy name is woman," he remembered thinking, without bitterness or regret. And actually feeling happy to have escaped from a long relationship relatively unscathed.

Well, that was then, and this is now, he mused. Last night it looked like he had found his soul mate. Even if he and Jennifer were not on the same page politically, he liked it that she had a mind of her own. Apparently she doubted the colonel's story at least as much as he did, though earlier she'd appeared reluctant to accept César's account about the plane. But why should she believe either one of them? César or Montero? It was best to remain open, objective. He was the one being irrational, probably because he couldn't stand the scumbag colonel, especially his silly, febrile advances toward her. Not that she took him seriously. From what he judged, the colonel attracted her about as much as a synagogue would attract a Muslim during Ramadan.

He chugged down his beer and then rolled over and grabbed the pillow, the one she had her head on last night. He could still smell her in the fabric, a sweet flowery smell like a spring meadow in heat.

Three hours later, in the middle of what he thought was a Buddy Rich drum solo, he awoke to Jennifer rapping on his door.

"Hey, you alive in there!" she yelled.

"Yeah, wait a second," he answered, gradually realizing where he was. "I'll meet you in the lobby. Give me five."

"Okay, but make it snappy," she laughed.

He sprang out of bed, brushed his teeth, ran his hand through his hair, patted it down, and was out the door.

In front of the hotel, he flagged down a taxi and crawled into the back seat after Jennifer. She was dressed casually in black jeans and a white blouse, but had left her Orioles cap behind. He was a little disappointed. He'd become accustomed to seeing her in her hat. It gave her a kind of Norman Rockwell charm.

Ten minutes later their beat-up taxi pulled up in front of a drab green police station, similar to the one where the car bomb had gone off that very morning. Two guards armed with assault rifles stood at the entrance. One of the guards motioned to the driver to pull ahead, away from the door.

Steve paid the driver before they got out of the taxi. As he closed the door, the guard who had waved the taxi on descended the steps of the police station.

"*Buenas tardes.* Can I help you?" he asked in Spanish in a serious but courteous tone.

"Yes, please. We have an appointment with Colonel Montero," Jennifer answered, also in Spanish, but with a thick gringo accent.

The guard gestured to them to follow him, and as they entered the station, he pointed to a desk in the lobby where an officer sat reading one of the daily tabloids.

Jennifer stepped up to the desk. "*Buenas tardes, señor.* Is Colonel Montero in? We have an appointment to see him."

Steve's eyes glanced behind the officer to a narrow hall that opened into a spacious courtyard. He could make out what appeared to be offices along both sides of the hall and a gate at the far end, most likely the location of the detainment cells.

"One minute, *señorita*," the officer replied and then stood up. "The colonel is in a meeting. I will tell him you are here." He strolled off down the hall toward the courtyard.

Steve stepped over to a huge map displayed on the wall to the left of the officer's desk. After studying the map, he turned to Jennifer.

"Here's where we were yesterday, before César took us up the river." He pointed to a dark green area close to a river. "And somewhere over here is where the plane crashed, I believe."

With his finger he traced a large circle around an area a couple inches away from where they were abducted.

"I think the plane went down about thirty kilometers from Tingo María. We traveled twenty to twenty-five kilometers before we were fired upon. So that means the site had to be very near."

Jennifer stepped closer to the map looking at the area where Steve had placed his finger.

"So the peasant family who saw the crash, if we can believe César that is, would have lived somewhere around here." She put her finger next to the word Machipa.

"That's correct."

"I know the colonel told us to forget going back out there because of the guerilla activity and what happened to the *campesinos* yesterday, but we need to find César. He is the only person who can lead us to the witnesses. So, maybe we're going to have to ignore the colonel."

"The problem is, César said the *campesinos* were too scared to talk. It might take a whole lot of convincing."

Just then Montero entered from the hall carrying a large manila envelope in his right hand.

"*Buenas tardes*," he said, smiling at Jennifer while giving Steve the cold shoulder. He stepped forward and kissed her lightly on the cheek.

"*Buenas tardes*," Jennifer replied, stepping back from the colonel and smiling. "I appreciate your letting us interview the prisoner. That's very kind of you."

"I was just sharing my report on the prisoner with the police commandant. The prisoner denies nothing in connection with the bombing this morning. Of course he refuses to talk at all. That's not important. One of my men has identified him. He also has a bullet wound in his left leg. It's from gunfire exchange."

"Is it okay to take some photos?" Jennifer asked.

Good move, Steve thought. It was better to ask, so not to anger the prick. He knew the military mentality. Soldiers had to ask for a clearance before they wiped their own asses.

"Yes, go right ahead. I also have some photos here, as well as the names of the dead *campesinos*, and some other details. The photos of the victims are not a pretty sight," he sighed, handing Jennifer the manila envelope."

"Thank you very much, Colonel," Jennifer said. "I'll make sure I get it back to you."

"This way please." Montero motioned them toward the hall as he ordered a guard to follow them. When they reached the iron gate at the far end of the open court, he nodded to the guard to unlock it.

Inside the holding area, the place smelled of urine and mildew. It reminded Steve more of a medieval dungeon than a prison. The gray walls had not been painted in years and the low wattage light bulbs barely illuminated the area. During the day, any light that entered this mausoleum came through the small windows positioned high on the back wall of the surrounding cells.

Montero, Steve, and Jennifer stopped before the door of one of the four cells.

"Open the door!" Montero commanded the guard sitting on a folding metal chair directly outside the cell. The guard had apparently been dozing. The puffiness around his eyes gave him away. He jumped to attention, saluted the colonel, and then began fumbling with his keys.

When the guard opened the door, Montero entered first. The pale light from outside the cell fell on his face hardening his features.

Steve and Jennifer followed him in. Huddled on a cot over in the corner, Steve could barely make out a shadowy figure.

"Scum, you have some visitors," the colonel said, strutting up to the figure and kicking the foot of the cot. He then swung around facing Jennifer and Steve. "I'll leave you with him. Take as long as you like. The guard will be outside if you need him."

The dark motionless figure waited for the colonel to leave and then in a low voice, not much above a whisper, said to Jennifer and Steve, "*Amigos, soy* Pépe."

Startled, Steve and Jennifer shot a glance at one another and then down at the figure swathed in darkness. With Jennifer close at his elbow, Steve inched toward the cot so he could get a better look at the person who had just spoken.

As they got nearer, they heard the springs in the cot squeak as the figure shifted himself, moving his stiff body into a small pale circle of light emanating from the window above. The soft light allowed them to make out the bruised and battered—but smiling—face of Pépe, César Montalvo's companion.

"Pépe?" Steve exclaimed in a hushed voice not loud enough for the guard to hear.

"*Silencio,*" he whispered, his stubby finger pressed to his lips. "I speak in English now. That way guard not understand me," he said, his hand resting on his leg wrapped in bloody gauze.

"Jesus, Pépe, what happened to you?" Jennifer exclaimed, a look of shock on her face. "Are you okay?"

"I hurt some. My leg," he said rubbing the dirty bandage. "Not much. Later, hurt go away."

"Pépe, did you and César bomb the *comisaria* this morning?"

"No, *señorita*, César not come with me. I have others help me."

"Does Colonel Montero know you are one of César's men?"

"No. He try make me say yes. But I don't talk."

"Where is César now?" Jennifer asked.

"I don't know," Pépe uttered softly, lowering his head and folding his leathery hands together cracking his knuckles.

"Montero claims César and some of his men killed forty-three *campesinos* yesterday afternoon."

"It is lie. Soldiers kill them. For this, we try to kill soldiers. I go with friend. His cousin die with others. I tell César I go kill soldiers. César say no, Pépe. Not good idea. But I go."

"Do you have proof about the killings?" Steve asked, looking Pépe sternly in the eyes.

"I no understand," he replied, sounding confused.

"*Pruebas?* Does César have *pruebas?* Proof?" Steve asked.

"César, he have proof. Two *campesinos*, they come to him and say what happen. Yes, they see everything. They go to César and tell him."

"But Pépe, why would the soldiers want to kill the *campesinos?*" Jennifer asked.

"They kill family with grandmother. They kill mother with children. They kill all of them. But soldiers not kill old man and his *nieto*, his grandson. They tell César what happen. They hide behind tree. See everything. They see *avion*, too, see plane."

"Wait a minute Pépe!" Steve said, trying not to speak too loud while controlling the adrenaline rush. "What do you mean they saw the plane? The one with the congressman?"

Truly astonished, Steve exchanged glances with Jennifer. This was unreal. These were the same *campesinos* that César had mentioned, the grandfather and his grandson that had witnessed the crash. The very *campesinos* they needed to find.

"*Sí*. The plane with American. He and grandson, they see."

"And because he saw the plane crash, the soldiers came looking for him and killed everyone?" Jennifer asked incredulously, her eyes glancing down at Pépe's knee and grimacing.

"Yes, *señorita*, this is what happen. The plane is not...*atentado*, how you say?"

"Attacked," Steve added.

"*Sí*, not attacked. The *gobierno* not want to tell truth. So they kill *la gente, los campesinos*."

"Look Pépe, you got to trust us. I believe you, but we need to find the *campesinos*, the old man who got away and his grandson. I know you want justice, or else you wouldn't have attacked the soldiers this morning. For this to happen, we have to find them."

"César, he know."

"How can we find César then, Pépe? You need to help us," Jennifer pleaded.

Pépe looked at Steve and then back at Jennifer, trying to read their expressions, trying to determine if the gringos could be trusted. Then after a long pause, "Go to Rosalina *restaurante*. It is *restaurante* near *Plaza de Armas*. Ask for Fernando Ruiz. Tell him I send you."

"He knows how we can contact César?" Jennifer asked.

"Yes, *señorita*. He find César for you. He know where César is."

"*Gracias*, Pépe." Steve placed his hand warmly on Pépe's shoulder. "With César's help we'll find the old man and his grandson, and then the people will learn the truth. That I promise you."

Pépe's face winced with pain as he shifted his body forward on the cot to take Steve's hand in his own.

"*Amigos*, I trust you. Maybe I not should trust you. But, I trust you."

Outside the police station a low bank of dark clouds formed over the distant hills where the sun had set minutes before. It was relatively quiet on the main avenue, except for a noisy car muffler in the distance and the laughter coming from across the street in the park where two young girls, about eleven or twelve, played with a volleyball, swatting it back and forth. Behind the giggly girls a young couple sat on a park bench making out.

Jennifer held on tightly to the envelope Montero had given her as she and Steve darted across the street.

"Jennifer, if the military murdered the *campesinos*, as Pépe says, they obviously will do anything to see to it the truth does not get out. That the crash wasn't caused by a missile."

"So now what?"

"We need to be extremely careful. If the military wiped out an entire village, they won't think twice about getting rid of us, if they see us as a threat."

Jennifer looked exhausted, and the heat and the humidity were contributing to her fatigue.

"So do you believe Pépe?" Steve asked.

"I'm beginning to believe Montero's story stinks. And that there are some higher ups involved who would like to escalate matters."

"Do you mean people connected to the American Embassy?"

"Maybe. Why would they restrict us from visiting the crash site? I mean Frank Pierce met us when we arrived and seemed more than willing to accommodate us. Right?"

"Sure looked that way."

"Then suddenly the American Embassy doesn't want us near the crash. Where is that coming from?" Jennifer asked.

"Your guess is as good as mine."

He suddenly thought about Congressman Kursten. Maybe the *campesinos* saw something they shouldn't have, and that's why the military silenced them.

"I think they're trying to hide something," he said. "What, I don't know. But it's beginning to look like the two *campesinos* do know."

"I've been running something through my mind. Bill Henkly contacted me about an opportunity to cover the story. I didn't go to him. He came to me. Then the Embassy even volunteered to provide transportation for me to Tingo María, on the condition that I promise to share my report with Henkly before I release it to Reuters. Remember? I told you about this yesterday."

"That's because they want to put their own spin on the event. Someone higher up must be calling the shots. That's why the State Department has taken over the investigation."

"Yeah, I think you're right. Those were my exact thoughts," Jennifer said. "They don't need us anymore, and they don't want us nosing around."

"And Frank Pierce tells everyone that his job at the American Embassy is 'civilian defense contractor.' Sure sounds like a spook to me."

"When I asked the colonel the other day about Pierce, he said he was from the American Embassy, though he passes himself off as working for an NGO. I asked the manager at the hotel about him, and that's what he said. He heads an NGO."

"Well, if he's not a spook, then I'm from Timbuktu."

"You're too damn pasty looking, not enough color," she smiled.

Then her expression suddenly changed. A dark cloud seemed to descend over her.

"Look," she said, serious now. "If you want, we can just throw in the towel and fly back to Lima tomorrow. Not to sound pessimistic, but there's a very good chance, if we start snooping around, that we may get in way over our heads. Already, this thing is far larger than we ever imagined, and that means far more dangerous."

"I say, we find César, and then take it from there. Pépe said we can reach him through this guy Fernando Ruiz at Rosalina's."

"So, you want to give it a shot?"

Did he want to give it a shot? Half of him said no. That he shouldn't get involved in anything political. Just say screw it and fly back to Lima with this lovely woman and forget about it. But he couldn't just walk away from what had happened in Machipa. There was no way he could do that. Walk away and forget about the bodies lying in the ditch, the back of their heads blown off. Many of them women and children.

"I say we do it. We find César and then we decide where to go from there. I'll check out this Fernando Ruiz. Pépe said that Rosalina's is right on the *Plaza de Armas*. So it should be a cinch to find. It's better that you don't tag along. I'm going to draw enough attention to my gringo self as it is."

"You're probably right. Look I'll go back to the hotel and go over what's in here," she said holding up the envelope Montero had given here. She then leaned forward, caught him by the sleeve, and kissed him on the cheek. "Hey, you be careful."

"Don't worry about me. I'll be fine."

"I'll see you back at the hotel later tonight. Don't be too late," she whispered in his ear in a low sexy voice."

Before she could step away, he grabbed her and kissed her passionately on the lips, holding her tightly to him. When he released her and drew back, he noticed her eyes all aglow, her cheeks rosier than usual, and her lips darker and more pinkish. The kiss appeared to have worked.

"Wow! You need to save some of that for later," she said, as she flagged down a cab.

"I will. If you promise to dig out that red dress for later. It's so damn sexy. If you do, I'll pay for dinner and drinks. Pretty please?" he pleaded, folding his hands together.

"Oh quit with those puppy dog eyes of yours," she laughed, as a taxi swung over to the curb. "To the hotel Esperanza, *por favor*," she said to the taxi driver in her sweet *gringa* accent.

"Si, *señorita*."

"Later!" Steve yelled and then waved as he watched her climb into the back of the taxi. As soon as the taxi pulled away, he hurried off in the direction of the *Plaza de Armas*.

13

Two long sidewalks crossed in the center of the *Plaza de Armas* slicing the tree-shaded park into four quadrants. A street vender had set up his stand and was busy selling *anticuchos de corazón*—skewed slices of beef heart, and *choclo*—cobs of corn with enormous kernels. A few meters away, a soldier, eating an *anticucho*, stood next to a young woman sitting on a small crate nursing her infant. She looked much older than her years. The harsh tropical sun had cracked and hardened her skin, and years of malnourishment had sucked the white from her teeth. She wore a black bowler hat with yellow bird feathers sticking out from its brightly colored band. Her cart displayed a plentiful stock of hard candies, cookies, cigarettes, chocolates, and artificial fruit juice.

Parked around the perimeter of the square were a few old cars and *mototaxis*. An old man in a faded polo shirt bent over the wheels of a battered red Toyota Corolla, wiping the hub caps clean of mud. The car had so many dents and scrapes, it looked like the neighborhood kids had taken sticks and used the car as a snare drum.

Two dark-skinned Indian girls sitting on a wooden park bench stopped chatting when Steve crossed the street. As he passed by them, they fixed their dark eyes on him. The taller of the two tried to get his attention.

"Hey, gringo. *A donde vas? Quieres que te acompañemos?"* Then in English, "You want company gringo?" she asked coyly.

"No, *gracias*," Steve said smiling back. Then in Spanish, "Some other night."

The girls laughed heartily. *"Si, otra noche, gringo."*

Across the main avenue from the plaza, Steve saw ROSALINA painted on a large sign above the door of a pastel blue building. The doors were wide open and the crowded interior of the restaurant stood fully exposed to the street.

As he approached the entrance, the sound of *boleros* playing over a radio intermingled with loud voices coming primarily from a bunch of rowdy drunks sitting at the tables in the center the room. To the right of the entrance, in a booth in the back corner playing cards, sat three old guys polishing off a bottle of pisco.

Steve walked in and sat down at the counter on the left. A grizzled, old man with a sagging face and watery eyes seated a couple stools to his right set his drink on the counter, swiveled his head around, and started staring at him like he was the first white guy he'd ever seen. A very tall Indian standing behind the counter looked up from his tabloid and then swaggered over. Steve's eyes fixed momentarily on a large scar that ran the length of his forearm.

"Si, *señor*?" he asked.

"A cold beer, please," Steve answered in Spanish.

The burly *mestizo* lumbered over to the freezer, lifted the lid, and took out a large beer. He jammed the bottle against the opener on the freezer and popped the top off. Then he returned and clunked the bottle down on the counter in front of Steve.

"Anything else?"

The drunken, raucous voices of the men behind him exacerbated Steve's unease. They sounded like they were quarrelling about something. He'd been in many local restaurants similar to this one, but he'd never felt so out of place, so like an intruder.

The big mestizo returned to the cash register and snatched up the newspaper he had been reading.

Steve looked behind him over his shoulder. As soon as he did, the three loud drunks sitting at the table in the center of the room looked up, stopped arguing for a few seconds, and then mumbled something and began laughing.

Steve filled his glass and then turned towards the guy at the cash register and said rather loudly, "Amigo, I'm looking for someone. Pépe Canchari said I could find him here. His name's Fernando Ruiz."

The big man looked up from his paper. He'd been leaning with his hands flat down against the counter top like he was about to do a set of pushups. His upper arms were as large as Steve's thigh.

"I'm Fernando Ruiz," he said coldly, locking his eyes on Steve's. "What do you want?"

"I would like to talk to you in private," Steve said with as much bravado as he could muster, hoping that the big mestizo couldn't smell the fear every pour in his body was exuding.

"About what?" he said, strolling over to where Steve sat and then leaning over the counter, his face only inches away from Steve's.

This spooked Steve even more. He tried to muster all the coolness he could. He quaffed down his beer and set the glass back on the counter, wiping the foam from his lips. He couldn't let this big fellow unnerve him anymore than he had. It was probably all bluster and bluff anyway, he tried to tell himself, though with little conviction

"César Montalvo," Steve said with all the pluck he had remaining.

The man stared at him with this cold look and said absolutely nothing while he ran his tongue over his teeth like he had a piece of food stuck there. Steve was beginning to feel like he had made a terrible mistake. The game he'd been trying to play changed suddenly to Russian roulette. The first wrong move would land him on a losing number, and what he stood to lose wasn't just the change in his pocket.

Fernando took his cold eyes off Steve just for a second, just long enough to quickly survey the room.

"Okay, gringo. We can talk out back," he said, nodding toward the rear of the building. "You'll see a door behind the restaurant. Just knock twice."

He rubbed the stubby growth on his face and then walked over and said something to a waiter who was clearing one of the tables.

Steve downed what remained in his glass and then tried to steady himself for what awaited him out back. Was he fucking crazy? He had to be insane to agree to meet Godzilla behind the restaurant. This guy was no one to mess with. And who was going to help him if he got his ass in trouble? It wasn't like he could step around the corner and holler for the police. In this part of town police were as rare as crazy gringos.

His knees felt spongy as he stepped around the corner into a dark, narrow alley between the restaurant and what looked like an all-night liquor store. At the back of the building, he could make out a door with a dim light shining above it. He moved cautiously toward the door and was about to rap on it when two men suddenly appeared behind him. They must have followed him out of the restaurant. One of them stepped quickly around in front of him and drew a knife and held it under his chin, tight against his throat. Steve's body stiffened like the corpse he thought he was about to become. One wrong move and he would be history.

"Don't do anything stupid, gringo," the man holding the knife said, and then slowly withdrew it from Steve's throat. "If you do, you'll be one sorry *cabrón*. Now move your ass!" he growled, as he shoved him toward the door.

Fernando stepped around in front of them and unlocked the door. As his knife wielding partner pushed Steve into the room, he stumbled and almost fell but managed to grab onto the table directly in front of him and upright himself.

A shabby light shade dangled from a wire in the center of the poorly lit room. From what Steve could see, the place served as a small one-room apartment furnished with a table, two chairs, a mini refrigerator, a dresser—with a portable TV on top, and a double bed.

Fernando motioned toward a chair. "Sit down gringo," he said, shoving Steve down on the hard seat.

Steve bowed his head and stared at his feet, waiting, not wanting to provoke Fernando in any way.

"Now tell me, what is it you want with César?" Fernando asked, leaning against the table with his large hands spread out over its top. "You lie gringo, and you die."

"I'm a journalist. Pépe said that you could contact César for me. He told me César could put me in touch with some important witnesses."

"Witnesses?"

"Yes, an old man and his grandson. They saw the military kill the *campesinos* right outside the village of Machipa. They also saw the plane crash, the one with the American senator."

"When did Pépe tell you this?"

"About an hour ago?"

Fernando took a couple of quick steps over to the dresser and yanked open a drawer. When he turned around he held an old Smith and Weston, what looked like a military issue. He raised it to Steve's head, pressed the cold barrel against his temple, and clicked the hammer back.

"*Cabrón,* Pépe is in jail! How did you talk to him, if he's in jail?"

Steve fought to keep his bowels from loosening. "I just talked to him!" he yelled out frantically. "I know he's in jail. I'm a journalist for Christ's sake! I also met with César and Pépe two days ago in the jungle. I'm investigating the plane crash. My partner and I went to César's camp. They arrested Pépe this morning after he bombed the police headquarters. He just told me about the *campesinos* less than an hour ago. He said César has evidence to prove the military killed the farmers and that Colonel Montero gave the orders."

All this came rushing out. Out of breath, Steve could feel his heart pounding in his ears while Fernando continued to hold the gun against his temple.

Fernando waited a few seconds and then released the hammer and lowered the gun. He lumbered over to the small refrigerator, opened the door, and returned with a beer. He stuck the top of the bottle in his mouth and removed the cap with his teeth. He then spat the cap on the floor.

"Look, gringo. Why should I believe your bullshit? You say you're a journalist. How do I know this? Because you have papers?"

"I don't know what else I can tell you. Like I said, I was at César's camp with my partner. You can ask César. I talked to him about the plane crash. Pépe was there to. César told me about the old man and his grandson who saw the crash. The authorities are claiming the *Senderistas* shot down the plan. César denies it. And then Pépe tonight told me that I should come here and ask you how I can find César. Look, I believe what César told me is true. That he had nothing to do with the plane. And nothing to do with the savage killings yesterday. But I need to see him. I'm staying at the Hotel Esperanza. Just ask César to contact me. He will tell you that we met."

"Okay, gringo. I will see that César gets your message. I will tell him what you have told me. But, gringo, if you want to live, don't try to trick me, or César."

He walked over to the door and opened it and then motioned to Steve that he was free to leave.

Outside Steve sighed deeply, shook his head, and said to himself under his breath, "Man, you're one lucky dude."

14

Steve had never had a knife to his throat, or a gun to his head, and in one night he was able to accomplish both, and it wasn't a good feeling. He crossed the street and sat down on an empty park bench, too emotionally drained to flag down a taxi. Meeting Fernando Ruiz, a Shining Path member or supporter, alone on an unfamiliar side of town far away from any protection, had been bordering on suicidal. Either that or he deserved to win the Most Stupid Journalist Award.

If Fernando Ruiz contacted César, and César agreed to arrange an interview with the *campesinos*, then what? Did he really have it in him to take on his own government? Because that's where it looked like it might be heading. Worse, he had this feeling that Kursten and the *campesino* killings were somehow connected. He was no Bob Woodword. And the *Lima Tribune* was not the *Washington Post*. Not even a pimple on the ass of the *Post*. So, who would be there for him when the shit hit the fan?

After a few minutes, he managed to get up from the bench and wave down a taxi. He instructed the driver to take him to the Hotel Esperanza. He needed to talk to Jennifer. Tell her what happened and get her take on what their next move should be.

When he approached the registration desk and asked for his key, the night clerk handed him a note from Jennifer. The note simply said that she'd be back late, that something unexpected had come up, and that she'd explain it all in the morning over breakfast.

That wasn't what he needed to hear at the moment. Not after tonight's near encounter with the Grim Reaper. If nothing else, he'd been hoping for at least a little sympathy, ideally offered over a large glass of Cabernet. Maybe even a little hanky-panky later. And then a quiet rest, falling asleep in her lovely arms and forgetting about the whole dreadful night.

"Did she say where she was going?" Steve asked, unable to disguise his disappointment.

"No, *señor*. She left with Colonel Montero."

"Colonel Montero?" What was the receptionist trying to do? Rub salt in his wounds? No, that was a stupid thought. He was just answering questions from a naïve gringo.

"Did she say when she'd return?"

"No, *señor*," the desk clerk replied sheepishly, apparently noticing the distress in his voice.

"*Gracias,*" he said, pressing his fingers against his eyeballs, feeling the tension building behind them, and then crumpling up the note and leaving it on the counter.

Outside the street was as deserted as his heart felt. For Christ's sake, he thought. What in the hell was she doing going anywhere with that grease ball murderer? Women. There was no figuring them out. They were mysterious creatures that could fill your heart one minute with precious treasures and the next minute make it feel like an empty tin box.

He was certain of one thing. He needed a drink. And not a Cabernet. A Scotch. No single nipper either, but a double straight down. And forget about on the rocks. He just wanted to erase this night altogether from his life.

He set off down the main avenue looking for that special place where he could drown his sorrows. As he crossed the intersection, he saw a red and blue neon sign with "Disco" on it and was instantly drawn like a moth to the flashing light.

At the front door a large black porter stood smoking a cigarette. Steve had observed that in Lima black porters seemed to be hot items. Every other hotel and disco in Lima had one. Apparently, they were hot items here as well. When the porter saw him approach, he stubbed his cigarette out on the sole of his shoe and then snapped to attention.

"*Buenas noches, señor,*" he said, smiling broadly. "Some real cute girls inside." He extended his hand toward the entrance. "Go in. It's free. No door charge."

"*Gracias,*" Steve said as he stepped into the narrow passageway, struggling for a moment to adjust his eyes to the darkness. Inside it was darker than a tomb, except for the swirling, pulsating light emanating from the dance floor and a few dim lights framing the bar mirror. Midway down the bar two shadowy figures sat leaning close together conversing. At least that's what it looked like at first. When Steve passed by them, he could make out a middle-aged man fondling a young girl who looked no more than eighteen. She had her hand on his cock, and the front of her blouse was opened exposing her breast while the guy's fingers played with her nipple. She smiled at Steve and then returned to business.

Three scantily dressed girls stood at the far end of the bar, their backs against the wall. Steve sauntered closer to have a better view of the lineup. They varied in age from eighteen to thirty.

He sat down on a stool about half way down the bar and ordered a scotch. While the bartender filled his shot glass, he glanced into bar mirror and smoothed down the top of his hair where a couple curls had sprung up. Suddenly he felt a light tug at his elbow. When he turned around, a girl in her early twenties smiled and sat down beside him. She had long dark hair and a cute round face with large brown eyes. Her lips really stood out. They were every Botox queen's dream, but hers were totally natural.

"Hi gringo," she smiled. Then leaning closer in, "Would you like to buy me a drink?" she crooned in his ear, her slender young hand rubbing his thigh.

"Sure thing sweets. What would you like?"

"I would like gin tonic with just *leetle* gin," she said, switching to English.

"So, you speak some English." Then to the waiter he said in Spanish, "Give her a gin and tonic, *por favor*, heavy on the tonic and light on the gin. And for me, another scotch."

"Yes, I took courses at institute in town. It's for my *yob*."

"For your *yob*?" Steve laughed. "That's good. What's your *yob*?"

"Why you laugh?" the girl said with a fake pout. "You're cute. I like you."

"I'm sorry. I'm not laughing at you. It's just your cute accent. So where do you work?"

"I'm secretary."

Yeah, probably was, Steve mused. Whoring helped pay the bills, besides offering a means of escape from a dreary life. Pure fantasy. First, find some sugar daddy with a deep pocket. Then pretend he cared about you for a few hours. Get him to buy you a few drinks- maybe even a dinner in a fancy restaurant, engage in a little hanky-panky, and call it a night.

"You have hotel close?"

Steve's eyes took a quick inventory of her well-endowed figure. "Would you like to dance?"

"Okay. And then later we go to hotel, yes?"

He pulled her gently by the arm onto the dance floor. Under the pulsating black light, she looked even sexier. Her breasts rose and fell freely beneath her thin rayon blouse as she shook her shoulders in perfect rhythm to the congas, brushing up against him, backing away, and then thrusting her pelvis forward provocatively.

The song by Santana, "Black and Magic Woman," was one of Steve's all-time favorites. Moving his shoulders in unison with hers, he moved in closer, placing his hands firmly around her thin waist. Gradually he worked his hands up along her ribcage, slipping them under her bra, cupping her firm young breasts, and giving them a hardy squeeze. She smiled at him approvingly and then leaned forward, brushing her loose dark hair against his cheek. "We go to hotel now?" she whispered in his ear.

The girl hung on Steve with her arm around his waist while he attempted to insert his key into the lock. For well over a minute, he fumbled with the key before noticing he'd been trying to insert it in an older lock, not the newer one positioned above the door handle. The drinks had made his head light, his feet unsteady, and his judgment absent without leave. Before departing from the disco, he'd downed five shots of scotch.

Once the door clicked open, he staggered into the room, the girl trailing behind him, her hand clinging to his shirt tail.

"Well, this is my room," he said. "What do you think? It's not the Hilton, but it does have a fine bed."

"I like it," she said, pulling him in the direction of the bed and then giving him a gentle shove, causing him to lose his balance and fall back onto the mattress.

Steve stared up at the girl who now stood over him at the foot of the bed. Without a moment's hesitation, she began slowly peeling down, beginning with her blouse.

"Hey gringo, I give you strip dance. You like?" she said, unbuckling her bra and tossing it to him.

"Yes, I like very much. Why don't you just dance yourself right over here," he said, struggling to get his shirt over his head and then quickly sliding his pants off and kicking them free.

She pulled her skirt down, let it fall to her feet, and stepped out of it. Next she put her fingers in the waistband of her black lace panties, and slowly, inch by inch, began lowering them as she wiggled her hips from side to side. Once she had the panties down around her knees, she stepped out of them, bent down and picked them up from the floor, and then began twirling them over her head laughing. When she was finished with her sexy little dance, she flung them toward Steve. He reached out to catch them but missed and almost tumbled off the bed.

She was laughing hysterically, as he clung to the side of the bed struggling to pull himself back up. She pranced over to him and then bent down to help him back onto the bed, her cantaloupe shaped breasts dangling like ripe fruit ready for the picking. She held her hands out and struggled to help pull him back onto the mattress.

Once she had him lying flat on the bed, she crawled cat-like on top of him. Then straddling him, she bent forward and pressed her breasts against his face, moving them from side to side across his five o'clock shadow.

15

Jennifer stood at the registration counter clicking her nails on the counter looking around for the receptionist.

"Hello! Anyone here?" she called out.

"Si *señorita*," the desk clerk said, emerging from a door behind the reception area.

"I buzzed Mr. Collins's room and no one answered. Is *señor* Collins in?"

"Yes *señorita*, he's still in his room."

"*Gracias.*"

She turned and headed down the brightly tiled hall toward his room. After knocking lightly at the door, she waited a few seconds and then when there was no answer, knocked a little louder.

"Steve? You in there?"

Steve rolled over in the bed and bumped against the girl cuddled up next to him. She was still asleep. "Shit," he said under his breath. "Get up. *Levantante!*"

Jennifer leaned closer listening, placing her ear against the door. Then she knocked again, but this time very loud. "Steve? You up?"

"*Que hora es? Tengo que irme,*" the girl blurted out.

Steve sprung out of bed and pulled on his underwear and grabbed up his pants.

"Jennifer, give me a few minutes. I just woke up."

"Take all the time you want, asshole," she said, and then strutted off toward the lobby.

Steve gathered up the girl's clothes from the floor, handed them to her, and then pulled her from bed in the direction of the bathroom.

"Here," he said reaching into his pants and pulling out his wallet. "Take this. And go ahead and use the shower if you like."

He handed her a few bills and then said, "But please, don't stay too long."

Then kissing her on the cheek, "Thanks for last night."

"Anytime Gringo," she smiled, and then closed the door to the bathroom.

After quickly throwing on his clothes, he leaned forward scrutinizing his image in the dresser mirror. He stuck out his tongue and examined the white ridges around its edge, and then ran his fingers through his tangled hair. He pinched and rubbed the skin directly under his eyes trying to erase the heavy shadows.

"Great fucking going, Casanova," he said out loud.

Jennifer sat at the dining room table sipping her coffee while reading through some documents and looking over photos.

Steve sheepishly made his way over to the table.

"God, I'm so hungry," he said. "I could eat just about anything."

"Didn't you get your fill last night?"

"Look, Jennifer, I had one hell of a night. You won't believe what…"

"I bet you did, partner."

"Yeah, well, I did," he said raising his voice, annoyed by her sarcasm. "I almost got a bullet in my head while you were out pumping Juan Carlos for…for who knows what."

"A bullet in your head?"

"Yes, a bullet in my head!"

"This was when you went to see Fernando?" she asked, looking up from the documents.

"Yes, first I thought I might get my throat cut, and then a few minutes later, I thought "wow," looks like I might have another option. Must be my night. Not the lottery exactly, but what the hell! A bullet in the head. Excellent second choice!"

Then pausing for dramatic effect. "It wasn't what you call a great night, unlike you might be thinking. Not unless your idea of a great night is getting the living daylights scared out of you by this crazy dude who is Quasimodo's look-alike, and his sadistic cutthroat sidekick who couldn't wait to carve out my Adam's apple."

Jennifer said nothing. She kept her eyes on the document in front of her, pretending to be going over the details. Steve could see that she was still pretty upset. What the fuck was he thinking last night bringing that girl back to his room?

"Look, I'm sorry," he said contritely. "When I got to the hotel last night and found out you weren't there, I kind of lost it. I really felt like I needed to see you, after all that had happened. Then I asked the counter guy if he knew where you were, and he handed me your note. He said he didn't know where you'd gone, but that you had left with the colonel. You can imagine how I felt."

She stopped reading and just shook her head, apparently trying to make sense out of what she was hearing. The good thing was she no longer looked like she wanted to scratch his eyes out, so Steve sensed she might be softening.

"Look, I'm not asking you to forgive me. I was stupid. Really stupid. I think the scotch didn't help either. Not that the scotch is any excuse for my behavior. Please, I don't want to destroy what we have," he said, his voice as wobbly as his legs as he sat down in the chair across from her.

She raised her head and looked straight at him. The injured look in her eyes let him know right away that she cared greatly about his silly fling, and that despite how stupid he had acted, she understood what had led him to make such a poor decision. She flicked the button on her pen up and down several times before deciding to speak.

"So, you spoke to Fernando?"

"Yeah," he sighed, relieved that she was willing to speak civilly to him.

She reached across the table and took his hand in hers.

He bit his lip and glanced down at his hands, embarrassed to look her in the eyes, like a child preparing to be lectured to by his mother.

She cocked her head to the side to try to establish eye contact with him.

"Hey Steve," she said softly. "It's just that…you know…that incident in your room this morning baffled me. Please, I don't want you to get the wrong idea. What you do is your own business. But God, Steve, how would you feel if you had caught me with someone right after you and I had, well, you know, had become intimate? I'm confused, to say the least. And I don't need confusion in my life."

"Look, I'm really sorry. Like I said, I was acting like a fool."

"You know, so much has happened so quickly in the past couple days that my head is spinning. Then last night and the colonel," she paused, having difficulty continuing.

"What about the colonel?" Steve asked, noting the troubled look in her eyes.

"Montero, I know for certain, isn't reporting the facts. Look at this." She slid the documents and photos across the table to him.

"Look closely at the details in the report."

Steve studied the report but found nothing unusual.

"I'm sorry," he said sounding perplexed, "but I don't see anything odd."

"He has the time of the killing of the *campesinos* at around 1:30 p.m."

"Okay?"

"Now look below under *Informes de Atentado*. The report says that César Montalvo directed the executions of the *campesinos*."

"Impossible," Steve said. Now he understood. "We didn't leave the rebel camp until late afternoon."

"That's why I asked the colonel to meet me last night. It wasn't a date, that's for sure. I remembered him mentioning that the Shining Path attack took place in the afternoon. I needed to check the time. Make sure the time recorded in the report was official. Not an error."

"You're so damn clever. So, he confirmed that the attack was in the afternoon?"

"Yes. He confirmed the time, and, in fact, said that he and his men exchanged gunfire with Montalvo shortly after the killings."

"Then he said he saw Montalvo himself?"

"That's what he said. But there's more. I had this note in my mailbox to call Frank Pierce. He confirmed what Colonel Montero had told us about keeping away from the crash site."

"When was this?"

"About the same time you left for Rosalina's to see Fernando. He said the State Department had taken over the investigation and they didn't want any reporters snooping around the crash site speculating on what might have occurred. Then he asked me what we had picked up on the crash."

"And?"

"I thought it was better not to mention that we'd met César Montalvo, and what Montalvo claimed happened to the plane. I told him we'd heard nothing, that we'd been delayed from reaching the site. And left it at that."

"Good going," he said, squeezing her hand.

"Steve, there's no way Pierce would believe César's story," she said sounding exasperated. "And it's obvious that the State Department, for whatever reasons, wants to keep whatever happened out there under lock and key, while Colonel Montero uses the incident against the Shining Path, maybe with some help from our Embassy."

"Well, it looks like César may have been telling the truth, now that we know Montero is full of it. At least we have something solid here that supports César's story," he said, handing the document back to her. "Making it look like the Shining Path killed

Senator Kursten was apparently important enough to wipe out an entire village."

"So, where to from here?" she asked, clearly flustered.

"We need to make a copy of this report."

"Are you scared?" He could see that she was trying desperately to read the expression in his eyes. "I sure am."

"Look Jennifer, like I said yesterday, we have to be very, very careful. We don't want anyone to know right now about César or any witnesses. Let's hope if we contact the witnesses, they're credible, and they saw what César claims they saw. Also that they'll be willing to testify. If we get that much, they'll be plenty of people back home asking questions. Once we have what we need from César, we're out of here. Back to Lima on the first plane. Colonel Montero's no one to play with. We need to put as much distance between him and us as we can or else we could end up like the *campesinos*."

"Last night the colonel really gave me the creeps. There I was sitting across from a mass murderer, trying my best not to panic while he ogled me."

"Well, if I have anything to say about it, the sick bastard is going to get what he deserves."

Then squeezing her hand once again he said, "About last night. It's important that you believe me, Jennifer. I am truly sorry. My head was not screwed on right. You really mean a lot to me. I wouldn't want to do anything to hurt you or jeopardize what we have going for us."

"Apology accepted," she said and then leaned across the table and kissed him on the lips. "You know, I've been a little tough on you, a little closed-minded. Not about last night, but about your politics. Henkly had something to do with that. He told me before I left Lima that I needed to watch you, that you tend to 'romanticize' in favor of the terrorists. That I needed to be careful about the slant you would put on things."

"Did he say anything else?"

"Well, yes. To support his comment about you, he mentioned a story you wrote years back for *The Atlantic*, the one I saw at your apartment. He told me it was a fabrication that cost you your job and ended up as a huge scandal for the magazine. He said in the article you lied about your interview with a Shining Path leader. That you never met him. That you made up the entire interview. Is that true?"

"Unfortunately it is. I put an interview together based on various conversations over the months I had had with various Shining Path rebels. I never interviewed the leader. I had arranged to meet with him, but he never showed up."

There, it was out. Now she knew. Now she was looking at the real Steve Collins. A washed-up loser.

"You know, had he showed, I bet he would have told it like you wrote it. How old were you? Early twenties, right?"

"Yeah, twenty-three about to be fifty," he chuckled ironically. "I was putting in fourteen hours a day. My career was my life. So much so that I felt I needed the story to break through. I'd already told my editor that I'd arranged the interview and that the piece was going to make the front page of the *New York Times*. Unfortunately, it did, but not the way I wanted it to."

"Well, I think it's time you forgive yourself, Mr. Collins. We all do foolish, regrettable things. What's important is that we learn from our mistakes, and don't repeat them. I know you meant good. Your heart was in the right place. You felt a need to tell the rebels' side, and so you took it too far, but you have more than paid for your youthful indiscretion," she said, running her hand over his crown, pushing down a few loose curls that had sprung loose.

"Thanks Jennifer. I appreciate your kind words." He did actually feel a little better. He had never discussed the incident with anyone. Although he didn't feel his confession exonerated him, Jennifer's acceptance and understanding did a whole lot to build his self-esteem.

"So, partner," she smiled, it looks like we wait, and hope we hear from César soon."

"At the restaurant last night, Fernando gave me the feeling that César would be in touch sooner than later."

"But he gave you nothing definite, right?"

"No. Other than the biggest fucking scare I've ever had."

The waiter walked over to their table and handed Steve a breakfast menu.

"*Buenos Dias, señor.* Would you like to order?"

"No, I'm fine, thanks."

The waiter turned to Jennifer. "And you, *señorita*? Would there be anything else?"

"No, *gracias.*"

Then turning to Steve, "You know what I feel like doing?" Her eyes suddenly lit up.

"No, what?"

"I feel like just forgetting about all this stuff and…" She paused and let the suspense build.

"And what?" he asked. He could tell by her mischievous smile that she had him where she wanted him.

"Seeing *Indiana Jones and the Last Crusade*. It's the afternoon matinee playing at the movie house across the town. Look, says so right here." She pushed her newspaper over in front of him with her finger on a photo of Indiana Jones snapping his whip. "You up for it?"

"Sure. I've seen it twice, but what the hell."

"I've seen it three times myself," she laughed.

"What do you say about meeting in the lobby around 3:30? I need to take a shower and wash the stench out of my hair. Then take a nap. I didn't get much sleep last…" He stopped, realizing he had just stuck a gun to his head and was about to pull the trigger.

"Yeah, I bet you didn't," she said grinning and shaking her head. "You were one bad boy!" She poked him in the rib.

"Ouch," he said, putting his hand to his chest. "And I thought you were the forgiving type."

"Just try to stay out of any mischief between now and this afternoon, especially any mischief involving the opposite sex."

"But you are the forgiving type, right?"

"It depends on the crime, buddy boy."

"Crime or misdemeanor?"

"In my book, you committed high treason."

"Forewarned and understood."

"Okay, 3:30 in the lobby," she said and then stood up from the table, leaned over and kissed him on the cheek.

16

Near the main entrance to the theater stood two small snack stands, and next to the curb, a decades old red popcorn machine. Steve walked up to the ticket window and gave ten *soles* to the ticket lady. She held the bill up to the light to see if the numbers changed color when she rotated the note slightly. Satisfied it was real, she handed him two tickets to the matinee.

"Would you like something, my dear?" he asked.

"Sure. That popcorn smells good."

Inside, the lights were still up and the screen still blank. The place was nearly empty, except for a few people sitting mainly in the center of the theater.

"Here, let's take these seats," Steve said, stopping about ten rows back from the front of the theater.

"Looks like we made it in time to catch the previews. Probably Bruce Lee and Van Damme flicks. Real kick ass stuff," Jennifer laughed. "I used to see those tacky films advertised in the local theaters all over Bogotá. I imagine it's the same here. Can't see what it is about those films that attract so many people. Jackie Chan's different. Now, he's funny."

Jennifer nestled down in her seat with her bag of popcorn on her lap, leaning her shoulder against Steve.

"This brings back memories," she said while popping a couple kernels in her mouth.

"How's that?" Steve asked, shifting in his seat to get comfortable.

"When I was a little girl I used to look forward to Saturday afternoons. My father would come by my mother's house in the morning and we'd go out to breakfast. My day with Dad. They divorced when I was about eleven."

"So you lived with your mother?" Steve wasn't sure why he even asked. Maybe because as a fatherless child, he thought she'd been lucky to have had a choice.

"Yeah, until I was fourteen."

"What happened?"

"Mom died of breast cancer."

"Sorry."

"That's okay. It was a long time ago," she sighed. "Anyway, Saturday was always a special day for me. Yep, my day with Dad. We had this special routine. He'd start out by buying a morning paper at the corner stand and then he'd hand me the movie section. I could choose whatever movie I wanted. But first we'd have breakfast at Donatelli's. My favorite place for breakfast. That place had the best pancakes. I'd order a huge stack of them and then spread an inch of butter on top with strawberry marmalade. And I'd always order a hot chocolate, of course. Um, makes my mouth water to think about those pancakes."

She rubbed her stomach to emphasize her point.

"As soon as I get back, my first breakfast out is going to be at the House of Pancakes. Not as good as Donaltelli's, but for a chain, it's not bad."

"So, what kind of movies would you choose?"

"My favorite films were police flicks, you know, Dirty Harry type movies, where the scumbags always get what's coming to them."

"Dirty Harry? Those movies are older than you are."

"Well, there was this cinema in the neighborhood that showed only classics. And Dirty Harry was very popular. I took my father to everyone that showed there. I think I had a crush on Clint Eastwood. Dad would usually fall asleep about a third of the way through the movie." She smiled nostalgically.

"Really? During a Dirty Harry movie? That's hard to imagine."

"Yeah, well, I always thought that was weird too, my own father falling asleep while Clint hunted down all the bad guys, serving up his own kind of justice, tidying up the world for us law-abiding folks who got screwed by the criminal justice system."

"You got that right. As I remember, Clint didn't think much of our legal system. He was your first modern day vigilante hero passing himself off as a policeman, delivering swift but merciless justice. Old Testament stuff, an eye for an eye. No mercy for the wicked. Moses with a Magnum."

"Dirty Harry was a character, alright," she agreed. "A real bad ass. Bigger than life. Not very believable really, unless you're an eleven-year-old."

"So, your dad didn't really get into the Dirty Harry flicks?"

"No, Dad really wasn't too impressed with Dirty Harry," she added with a note of sadness. "Bigger than life characters and Hollywood heroics did nothing for him."

"Why was that?" Steve asked, noticing that she had become more pensive than usual.

"He was a cop, a detective," she said and then glanced up quickly at the ceiling and bit her lip. "I think, without really knowing it, I chose those movies to let him know I cared about what he was doing."

"Is he retired now?"

"He was killed when he walked in on a robbery at a 7-Eleven. There were two of them, one inside and the other outside. The guy who shot him came through the front door after dad had drawn on the guy's partner holding up the clerk. I was twenty-three years old. I'd just celebrated my birthday the night before at Dad's house."

Although the light was faint, Steve could see that her eyes had begun to well up with tears.

"I'm really sorry to hear that Jennifer," he said taking her hand in his.

She wiped her eyes and quickly changed the subject. "So, you've seen this flick twice, huh?"

"Yeah. Remember the Nazi gal? A double agent, as I recall. Indiana gets in real deep with her. Man, she really does this number on his head."

"He gets in deep alright, but he figures things out soon enough. And then gets over her, just like that," she said snapping her fingers.

"Yeah, well my take on it is that he was more in love with that bod of hers than anything else. Once he realized that, she was easy to crack."

"Even so, Indiana's not the kind of guy to end up with a broken heart. He's too damn tough to let a dame get the best of him."

"'He's too damn tough to let a dame get the best of him?' That sounds like a line from Bogart."

He reached in his bag for popcorn, but his hand was too large so he ended up splitting open its side, spilling the kernels all over his lap.

"My poor clumsy baby," she smiled, brushing the popcorn onto the floor, and then leaning over and kissing him on the lips.

As their lips touched, the lights in the theater began to dim and the projector illuminated the screen. Once he'd settled back in his seat, he glanced over at Jennifer. Patterns of light and shadow flicked across her face as she stared up at the screen. The disorienting effect of the staccato flashes gave her a kind of impermanence, as though she was there beside him but had not fully materialized. She reminded him of one of those characters from *Star Trek*, like she had been beamed into the theater but all of her particles hadn't regrouped. For a second, he had this unsettling feeling she wasn't real.

As he leaned his head back in the seat trying to clear the strange thought from his brain, the projector suddenly stopped and the theater went pitch black.

"What happened?" Jennifer asked, alarmed, clutching his arm.

"Probably just the projector bulb. That's my guess. Could be the projector itself, though. Remember, we're in Peru, the land of the unpredictable and hardly fixable."

"Hey! Watch yourself! You're starting to sound like an Ugly American," she teased.

"I hope not. As crazy as it might sound, I actually love this place. Not Tingo, mind you, but most of Peru."

"God, you've been here so long, you must feel half Peruvian."

"Well, that's pushing it some," he laughed.

"Is it really? From what you've showed me, you fit right in."

He stretched out as much as he could in the small space he had between the closely arranged rows.

"This could be a long wait, you know. Cozy seats though."

Just then the doors in the rear of the theater opened and the heads of the audience became dimly visible. The usher took a few cautious steps down the center aisle, his flashlight beam bouncing through the darkness, providing just enough light to make out his outline.

"*Hay un apagòn. Pueden salir y presentar sus boletos en la ventanilla del salón,*" he called out.

"Did you get that?"

"Yeah, he said something about the power going out and presenting our tickets at the ticket window."

"Oh well, welcome to Peru," he said, and then stood up to leave.

"Hey, wait a second buddy boy. I have an idea, something we can do for entertainment," she said, grabbing onto his shirt tail and abruptly halting his egress.

"What did you have in mind?" he asked, guessing where this might be going and crossing his fingers and hoping he was right.

"You know one thing blackouts are known for?" she said, sliding her hands around his waist.

"I think so. But in a theater?"

"And why not?" Her hands moved slowly up to his chest to the tuft of hair at the base of his neck. She gently twisted a strand between her thumb and index finger. Her fingers then moved down to the opening in his shirt where her fingers closed around the top button. She began slowly unfastening his shirt front while kissing him on the neck and chest.

As she did so, Steve breathed in the sweet smell of jasmine on her neck and in her hair. He slid his hands behind her, up under her shirt, and then began working them upward until his fingers made contact with the metal clip on her bra strap.

The usher had closed the doors and now only a few thin rays of light slid through the cracks that framed the doors.

"I'll bet not many people have made love in a theater," she cooed, and then ran her tongue over his cheek.

"I know I haven't. And I doubt that Indiana Jones has either."

"I'm offering you the chance to upstage your hero."

"This is crazy you know." He said this while popping loose her bra strap.

"So, are you feeling a little crazy?" she whispered, unbuttoning the last button of his shirt.

"Around you? Crazy can't begin to describe what I feel."

He slid his hands from behind her back around to her front. Then he grabbed her breasts in both hands, squeezed them softly, and began moving his fingers back and forth across her hard nipples.

"Great, I'm in the mood for crazy," she purred in his ear.

Jennifer shot a quick glance behind her. The place was pretty much pitch dark and not a soul around. She quickly pulled her skirt up around her waist and pulled down her soft cotton panties.

Steve wiped the sweat from his forehead with the back of his arm and then lifted the bottom of his seat, folding it back to allow more space. As his heart raced wildly, he grabbed onto Jennifer's thin waist and navigated her around in front of him, pressing her bare buttocks up against the hard seat back.

"I'm all goose bumps," she said and began kissing his neck.

He moved his hands over the soft curves of her thighs and her smooth, firm derriere. If heaven existed, his heart told him, he had found it right here in this dumpy old theater. *The mind is its own place, and in itself can make a heaven of hell, a hell of heaven.* How right Milton was. The place didn't matter. You could discover heaven anywhere.

He leaned in closer, trying to read what was in those beautiful dark eyes. What he saw might have passed itself off as pure lust, had he not looked closer. There was hunger there, and no doubt, lust, but underneath that hunger and lust he saw a willful surrender that had love written all over it.

When they finished, they were both dripping sweat. Panting, Jennifer laid her head on his shoulder. Steve felt a slight tremor run through her limp body as her heart beat wildly against his arm.

He kissed her gently on the mouth and then bent over and picked up her panties. "I think you might need these."

She took them from him, smiled coyly, and slid them back on without uttering a word. Her reticence surprised him. She always seemed to have something to say. Perhaps she felt a little embarrassed about her forwardness, her sexually aggressive behavior, though he saw no reason for her to feel ashamed.

A few moments later when they were standing in front of the theater, he asked her if anything was bothering her.

"No. I'm fine," she said, squeezing his hand. "That was pretty wild. I'm not sure what came over me. I hope you don't get the wrong idea."

"The wrong idea? About you? Never," he said, taking her head in his hands and looking into her soft dark eyes. "You know, you've put a lot of sunshine in this gray life of mine. I'd make love to you in broad daylight on Fifth Avenue if you asked, and be damn proud to do it."

"Thanks," she smiled. "I don't think I'll ask you to do that, but I'll remember the offer. What I think I need now more than anything is a cool shower. It looks like you could use one as well." She kissed him on the tip of his nose and then took him by the hand and led him toward the curb where they flagged down a taxi.

17

Back at the hotel Esperanza, Steve and Jennifer stood at front of the registration desk waiting for the desk clerk to hand them their room keys. The short ride in the *mototaxi* back to the hotel had raised her spirits. Steve had joked with her about returning to see the flick tomorrow and paying the guy that ran the projector to shut it down.

"Dinner Later?" Steve asked.

"So soon after dessert?" Jennifer laughed.

"We could have dessert again, after dinner."

"You do have real sweet tooth now, don't you?" she said pinching his side.

"*Buenas tardes*," the desk clerk said, passing Jennifer and Steve their keys across the counter.

"Oh, *Señor* Collins, there's a note for you." He withdrew a slip of paper from the key box and handed it to Steve.

Steve unfolded the paper. The only information on it was an address and time, and the name Fernando. He handed it to Jennifer.

"Is it about César?"

"I don't have any other reason for meeting Fernando. And I hope he doesn't either." He tried to chuckle, but wasn't very successful. After his near fatal encounter the night before, if he never saw Fernando again, that would be one time too many.

"Should I come with you?"

"I don't think it would be a good idea. They might become suspicious if you were to just show up. And I really don't want to upset anyone. When I mentioned talking to Pépe, Fernando had no idea that I had talked to him after his arrest. He thought I was lying. He almost did me right there without thinking twice about it."

"I could hide out close by. Then go for the police if I needed to."

"No, I'll be okay. Believe me, you wouldn't find any cops in that neck of the woods anyway."

"Okay. But do be careful."

"I will," he smiled, then paused and said, "You know, we're damn close now. I can feel it. It's all up to César Montalvo now. If he comes through, we'll know very soon what happened to the plane and what went down in Machipa."

"And why shouldn't he cooperate? If he's telling the truth and we expose Montero, it serves his interests."

"César isn't what troubles me though. I think he'll come through."

"So what troubles you?"

"Well, we're not really sure about what role the Embassy's playing in all of this. Ambassador Wenton might be part of a scheme to lay the blame on the Shining Path."

"One thing at a time, Detective Columbo. First see if César's willing to help us, and if he can produce credible witnesses."

Steve placed his arms around her waist and then leaned backwards, balancing his weight against hers. "I'm going to jump in the shower. Look, it's about an hour's bus trip to San Ramon, the place Fernando wants me to meet him. And it's 6:45 now. So, if it isn't too late when I get back, I'll stop by your room and let you know how everything went. Okay?"

"It won't be too late. And, you be careful," she said, furrowing her brow and then leaning into him and kissing him lightly.

As soon as Jennifer entered her room, she quickly opened her purse and removed her cell phone. Then she hurried over to the window and pulled back the curtains just a crack and peered outside. As soon as she saw Steve cross the street and turn the corner near the bodega, she switched on her phone. To her dismay it was dead. She'd forgotten to charge the battery last night. She needed to get to a payphone. She remembered seeing one yesterday in the open market.

About ten feet from the fruit stand, she saw a public phone. She hurried over to an old woman near a fruit stand and asked her for two mangos. The old woman weighed the mangos and told her the price. Jennifer reached into her purse and took out a crinkled bill. The woman withdrew two coins from her apron and handed them to Jennifer.

"*Tome*," she said to Jennifer. "*Gracias.*"

"*De nada. Aqui, Guardalo*," Jennifer replied, telling her to keep one of the coins. The other one she needed for the phone.

She stepped behind the old woman's cart over to the public phone and deposited a coin in the slot and then waited.

"Hello, this is Barnz. You said to keep you updated."

"Okay, and…?"

Jennifer looked behind her over her shoulder. "Well, at the present, nothing on the subject's whereabouts, but Collins went to meet with a contact. I should have something real soon."

"Okay. Just let me know when and where."

"By the way, I used Montero's report to convince Collins that the colonel was lying. It was a way of drawing him in more."

"Lying? How's that?"

"The time entered on the report proves the colonel could not have seen César Montalvo near Machipa. There's no way Montalvo was involved. Collins and I were with him at the time."

"You need to keep quiet about your encounter with Montalvo then."

An old street beggar, who had stolen up behind her, nudged her elbow. Startled, she turned around and found his crusty palm thrust in her face.

"Por favor, señorita," he half sang. He smelled of piss and cheap booze. The front of his pants had a large slit, exposing part of his genitals.

"No tengo ningún cambio," she said, and then waved him off like some pesky mutt before returning to her conversation.

"I don't like this. If Montalvo had nothing to do with the *campesinos'* deaths, then you know what that means?"

"No, I don't. And neither do you. As far as we're concerned, Colonel Montero's story stands," he said with ire in his voice, wanting to end the conversation there and then.

"The colonel claims the *campesinos* were killed because the terrorists believed they were traitors. He told me that two of the women killed had ties to the mayor of San Martin, the same mayor the Shining Path assassinated a few months ago. Is this information correct?"

"That's not really my department. Or yours. Our mission is to get Montalvo. And it looks like that's going to happen. Your idea to hook up with Collins is going to pay off. Good job."

"Thanks," she said, and then swallowed hard. "I'll get back to you soon as I have more."

"Alright. And make sure to get rid of the report you showed Collins."

After she'd hung up the phone, she stood staring at its black casing as though its smooth plastic surface held an answer to the feelings churning inside her.

How many of the forty-three were children she wondered? She suddenly felt dizzy and out of breath. She had read about cases of genocide. But this was the real thing. Not only the real thing; she was privy to details that implied the Peruvian army was behind the killings and the CIA knew it but was withholding information.

In Colombia she had gathered intelligence while writing short pieces for Reuters. That was fine. But this wasn't the same. She was seeing things now from an entirely different perspective. She didn't doubt that the rebel movement in Peru had to be quashed. Communism, and especially this crazy Maoism the rebels were preaching, was a threat to the free world. They couldn't allow it to spread. But forty-three dead *campesinos*. Was she to overlook what really happened? Pretend like it never occurred?

She leaned against the side of the building waiting for her head to clear and her breathing to return to normal.

Across the street a young couple in their early twenties sat on a park bench laughing. They were licking fruit flavored ice cones called *raspadillas*, happy and totally removed from all the bullshit going on around them.

How she envied them. She was right at the center of some very ugly business. Suddenly horrid images of the dead *campesinos* lying in a trench along the side of the road flashed through her brain. Old people, mothers, children, lying there with the backs of their heads missing. Cold, stiff corpses.

She felt sick. Still leaning against the side of the building, she took a handkerchief out of her purse and held it up to her mouth, fearing she might puke. She was facing the first real crisis in her short career and wondering if she would survive it.

18

About a hundred meters off a muddy jungle road a few kilometers outside of Tingo María, César stepped out of one of three beat up old cars. They had planned to break Pépe out of jail and decided on seven in the evening, when the police station had only a few guards on duty. Also, at this time of year, it would already be dark.

César had attempted to rescue two prisoners about a year ago at the police headquarters in Pucallpa, but the rescue had been an absolute disaster. He had the misfortune to pick a time when a military patrol decided to pass through town. He lost three men and barely escaped himself. He would not make the same mistake this time. He would position four men with cell phones around the possible routes that led to the police station. As a decoy, his men would hit the police station on the opposite side of town five minutes before staging Pépe's break out. The dynamite blast would be certain to draw attention away from their real target.

César walked around to the rear of José's car, opened the trunk, removed the cover from the tire well, and checked the dynamite. The rigging looked fine. He shut the trunk, looked at his watch, and then motioned to his men that it was time. As César and three of his men entered the lead car, José motioned to eight heavily armed rebels to pile into the other two cars.

The eight men watched César's car bucket out from the dirt road onto the highway. Instead of heading out behind him, they waited at the side of the road. As César's car picked up speed, they stared at the car's rear lights growing smaller and smaller until they became two tiny red dots and then disappeared completely from view.

José looked at his wristwatch, waited thirty seconds, and then looked again. It was time. He started his engine and pulled onto the highway. The other car followed a short distance behind him. José's destination was the police station across town. He was in charge of setting off the dynamite. The other car would join César and be used to set up a surveillance point.

Back in his cell, Pépe lay on an army blanket stretched over the springs of a small metal cot. As he heard the guard approaching, he raised himself stiffly, his hand resting on his injured leg. The paunchy cop, a sergeant in his late thirties, carried a plate of frijoles and rice in one hand and a tin cup in the other.

"Asshole! Your food!" he barked out.

Pépe rose up slowly from the cot and shuffled over to the door, dragging his injured leg behind him. He gripped the bars of his cell door and then spat on the floor, fixing his eyes fiercely on the guard's.

The sergeant set the food and drink down on the metal fold-up chair directly across from Pépe's door. Then in one lightening move, he snatched his club from his waist, swung around to the cell door, and smashed the club down against Pépe's fingers.

"AYAAA! Son of a Bitch! You fucking *pendejo*!" Pépe screamed out, unable to control the pain.

Then the sergeant turned back around and took the tin cup from the chair. "Your drink, pig," he said, tossing the water in Pépe's face. Then with a look of pure malevolence, he lifted the plate from the stool, and tilting it slightly, slid it through the bars and released it. "And your food." The plate of rice and frijoles splattered onto the floor at Pépe's feet.

"Go fuck your mother!" Pépe said, his eyes riveted on the guard while he raised his smashed and bleeding fingers to his lips and began sucking on them. He spat the blood from his fingers onto the floor while his face transformed itself into an expression of pure loathing.

Two blocks away, César's car pulled to a stop at the curb. The driver, a young boy, about eighteen, killed the motor and slumped down behind the wheel waiting while César and three other men, all in ski masks and armed with assault rifles, emerged from the car.

Two policemen stood guard in front of the entrance engaged in lighthearted conversation. The fat sergeant appeared in the entrance and said something to one of the guards who laughed loudly and then took out a pack of cigarettes and handed the sergeant one. He lit the cigarette and then turned to go back into the station when a large blast from across town suddenly froze him in his steps. The two guards stiffened, looked at each other in surprise, and then watched as the sergeant rushed into the station.

The sergeant shouted to the policeman at the desk to call across town to see if the other station had any information about the explosion. The two policemen standing guard at the door came inside and stood next to the sergeant waiting for instructions. He told them to go back to their post while he waited for news from across town.

César glanced at his two comrades, pointed his index finger at his watch, and then checked his cell phone. Had there been any patrols in the vicinity, one of the four rebels placed strategically nearby would have sent a text-message. César nodded to his men. The time was now! He yanked a dynamite stick from his waistband and took out a lighter from his shirt pocket. They were only about twenty meters away from the entrance of the police station. He flicked the lighter on and held it to the wick and waited a second for it to catch. When it did, he gave the dynamite stick a hearty toss at the entrance of the building.

The guards saw the stick fly through the air and strike the concrete floor between them before skidding into the station. Their faces froze with panic as they stared at each other not sure what to do next. An identical thought must have entered their minds at the same instant. As they turned to rush from the building to save their own asses, they were too late. Barely in motion when the dynamite detonated, the powerful blast hurled them into the air and deposited their tattered, bloody bodies a few meters from the entrance to the station.

Across town a heavy exchange of gunfire had commenced between several policemen and four of César's rebels under the command of José. The car blast the rebels had set off moments before in front of the police station had blown the front doors off the car and shattered its windows. A policeman lay dead on the sidewalk among the debris. Right after the explosion, two policemen ran out of the station to see what had happened, not realizing that they had made themselves perfect targets. José opened fire on them, killing both of them instantly.

To the rebels' surprise, a dozen or more policemen from inside and around the corner of the building began firing back at them. Two cops scampered from behind the police building, taking refuge behind two large trees about fifteen meters from the entrance to the station. José had not expected so many cops at this hour of the evening. Apparently there had been a meeting that had kept them later than usual.

He and his comrades decided to dart for cover behind a delivery truck parked a few meters from the corner store close to where the getaway car was waiting. José told his men to get ready to make a run for the car while he gave them cover. They knew the plan. If they made it to the corner, then they would cover for him.

José decided to focus his fire on the two policemen behind the trees, since they were more dangerously positioned than the policemen inside the station. He leapt up above the hood line of the truck and fired off a full clip, taking out one of the cops, but at the same time caught a bullet in his right shoulder. The cop that he had hit stumbled forward spasmodically firing into the air before collapsing face first on the ground, his arms splayed out in front of him and his finger still on the trigger of his P90.

It was now or never. José knew he had to make a run for it. He looked at his blood soaked shirt. His shoulder was numb where the bullet had ripped through his flesh, and he felt the warm blood spreading out into the fabric of his shirt. He dashed out from behind the truck and hurled himself in the direction of the escape vehicle.

As soon as his comrades saw him break for it, they turned their weapons on the front of the police station firing a barrage of rounds. The station walls offered ample protection for the policemen, so the rebels' cover proved largely ineffective. As soon as the police saw José dart from behind the truck, they opened up with everything they had, keeping below the station windows, or to the side, out of range of the rebels' bullets. They fired so fast and furiously that the rebels could only stick their guns around the corner of the building and fire off blindly, praying that their bullets would provide some cover for their comrade.

Before José could reach the midway point, several bullets ripped through his back and exited through his chest. His arms flew out in front of him, as though desperately reaching for a life line to reel him in, and then his body struck the pavement with a thud, his weapon slamming to ground next to him.

From behind the corner wall, his two comrades shot a look at each other and the decision was made. It would be foolish to stay a second longer. Out of range from the policemen's gunfire, they sped toward the getaway car. The driver had the rear door open for them as they dove into the backseat like two frightened rabbits into the safety of their rabbit hole.

The car fish-tailed down the road as two cops emerged around the corner firing off shots striking the rear end of the car and shattering its rear window. Seconds later the car swung hard to the right down a side street and disappeared.

A rebel stood near the entrance as César and two of his comrades hurried inside. The lobby was enveloped in a thick gray smoke. As they entered the room, César and his men covered their mouths and noses with their shirt sleeves. On the floor in the middle of the lobby, they saw two policemen lying motionless, apparently dead from the impact of the blast.

César walked up to them and poked them with his foot. When there was no response, he stepped over their bodies and entered the long narrow hall with his men following on his heels.

"Pépe! Where are you!" he shouted and then waited a few seconds. "It's César!" he hollered again, and then began coughing. He quickly covered his mouth and nose with his shirt sleeve.

"Here!" Pépe yelled back.

César hurried off down the hall in the direction of Pépe's voice. Coughing and rubbing his eyes, he searched through the smoky haze and then saw Pépe kneeling and leaning against the bars. A few minutes before, he had been sprawled on the floor pressing his head against the tiles to keep from breathing in the smoke. He had ripped off a piece of his shirt, balled it up, and was holding it over his mouth and nose.

"Move out of the way! I'm going to break the lock!" he shouted to Pépe.

"You don't need to," Pépe replied coughing. "They're on the wall over there." He pointed to his right to where a ring of keys hung from a nail.

One of César's men snatched the keys and tossed them to César. He thrust one of the keys into the door lock and turned the key, but the lock would not click open. He tried another key and this time got lucky. He threw the door open and rushed into the cell. Bending down, one arm covering his nose to filter out the smoke, he grabbed Pépe around the waist with his free arm. Pépe threw his arm over César's shoulder and around his neck for support as César helped pull him up from the floor.

As they entered the lobby, Pépe noticed the fat sergeant lying prostrate in the corner. Because of all the smoke in the room, César and the others had not seen him when they rushed in. His leg had been ripped wide open from the explosion. Lying in a pool of blood and groaning weakly, he moved his hand down to his shattered leg. One of the rebels standing over him, looked at César for approval and then aimed his assault weapon at the man's head.

"No! Wait!" Pépe shouted. He let go of César's waist, and then gritting his teeth, hobbled over to the rebel. He motioned to

125

him to hand him his assault rifle. Taking the rifle, he jabbed it into the fat cop's side, forcing him to roll over so he could see his face. The sergeant began to moan loudly, but when he saw Pépe he went silent. His whole body stiffened and his eyes shot wide open in pure panic.

Smiling, Pépe gazed down at him and saw nothing but pure terror in his eyes.

"Please! I beg you! Don't kill me!" he pleaded.

"And why not pig?" Pépe responded, no longer smiling. He raised the weapon slowly to the guard's face while he tried to bend the bloody finger of his right hand around the trigger, but his finger was too swollen. He shifted the heavy weapon to his other hand and said, "Now I give you back your own medicine, *pendejo*." He squeezed the trigger and there was a loud explosion as blood splattered the wall. Handing the rifle back to the rebel, he slowly raised his injured hand and sucked on the end of it drawing some blood. He looked down at the faceless inert body and then spat, "*Hijo de puta!*"

"*Vàmonos!*" César said grabbing Pépe around the waist. "Let's get out of here!"

19

Steve didn't have a clue as to what awaited him. He was off to meet César in San Ramon, a *pueblo joven* on the outskirts of Tingo María. That was the extent of what he knew. Maybe he had a death wish. Why in the hell else would he be heading for a local slum to meet a notorious terrorist?

He showed a guy at the corner store the address, and the man told him that he knew the area but not the street. He then warned him that Villa Ramon was notorious for its street gangs, so he better stay alert.

Great, Steve thought.

He then told Steve the easiest way to get there would be to take any of the blue and white buses that had *aeropuerto* written on the side. As Steve was stepping away, he yelled out, "Here comes one now!"

"Thanks!" Steve called back.

When the driver saw Steve's hand go up, he hit the brakes and the bus screeched to a stop. He hopped aboard, squeezing his way to the center of the aisle through the tightly packed bus. He hung onto the chrome hand rail trying to keep his balance as the bus rattled and thumped down the road. His left hand managed to move his wallet from his rear pocket to his front, making it tougher to pick pocket.

About thirty minutes later, the bus began winding slowly up a clay hillside on the outskirts of town, its landscape as barren of vegetation as a strip mine. It was like a giant's hand had scraped the fertile jungle of its greenness, leaving behind a huge, ugly scar. Steve got the impression that the area used to be a landfill. Every couple minutes the bus would stop to pick up and let off passengers and then lurch forward up the hill, belching smoke and grinding through its lower gears.

Eventually the potholed asphalt street turned into a rutty dirt road with intersecting streets every hundred meters. It was not a pretty sight, what he could see of it under the dim street lights. Over half the homes consisted of unfinished shacks erected on barren, litter strewn lots. Simple makeshift abodes constructed of brick, cardboard, tin, and wooden slats, the kind of cheap wood slats used to manufacture fruit crates. There was not one tree, plant, or blade of grass. This vast godforsaken area looked more like a littered moonscape than an urban district.

The bus screeched to a halt and then dropped off two men and an old woman carrying a bag stuffed with odds and ends. Before the old woman could descend the bus steps, Steve tapped her on the shoulder and showed her the slip of paper with the address.

"Excuse me, *señora*. Could you help me please? Do you know this place?"

"*Sí, señor*, it's about two blocks away. Go up the hill and turn left," the old woman croaked out in a voice as thin and coarse as the threadbare bag she had at her side. She pointed up the road. "It's the street near the Fanta sign."

"*Gracias señora*," he said and then moved in the direction she'd pointed out.

As Steve began his ascent up a narrow dirt street, he realized that it had taken him much longer than he'd thought to arrive. Standing under a street light, he looked down at his watch. It was nearly nine o'clock. The surrounding darkness made him more uncomfortable by the second.

As he continued up the hill it grew even darker as the street lights disappeared altogether. He noticed that only kerosene lanterns or candles lit the interior of the houses. Electricity had not reached this far up the hillside.

A scruffy dog, skin stretched tightly over its protruding rib cage, rose up from the doorstep of one of the houses and followed at Steve's footsteps. Fortunately, the dog was not aggressive and stayed with him for only about half a block before turning and wandering off.

He was thinking about turning back himself when directly ahead he saw an unpainted brick structure with the same number on it that had been written on the paper. At last, he thought. Now the drama begins.

He lifted his arm to rap on the door, but before his knuckles made contact, the door sprang part way open and Fernando's face appeared. His cold hard eyes fixed on Steve's for a couple of seconds before darting down the street to the bottom of the hill.

"You were not followed, no?" he asked, as his eyes drilled into Steve's.

"No. I'm…I wasn't."

Fernando opened the door and motioned him inside.

A kerosene lantern hung suspended from the ceiling. The wick had been turned down so low that the lamp barely lit the room. Directly below the lamp was a wooden table with four chairs. To Steve's right, underneath a plaster crucifix tacked on the wall, sat a dark figure. He could not make out his features.

"César? Is he here?"

"He will arrive soon," Fernando replied flatly.

The figure who had been sitting in the shadows rose and stepped forward. He was a short bearded man with blue jeans and a red shirt. The same fellow who had held the knife to his throat. Without saying a word, he brushed by Steve and disappeared behind a plastic drape that hung between their room and a room in the back. Seconds later, he returned with a large bottle of beer and one small glass. He poured the beer into the glass, gulped it down, and then filled it again.

"I am Bernardo. Would you like *cerveza?*" he asked holding the glass out to Steve.

"*Gracias,*" Steve replied, his voice as tight as a guitar string tuned several octaves too high and ready to snap. "My name's Steve Collins."

Steve quaffed the beer and then passed the glass back to Bernardo, who then passed it to Fernando. Fernando filled it, raised it to his lips, and was just about to drink when they heard a shrill whistle outside the door.

"It's César!" Fernando said.

He set the glass on the table and stepped over to the front door. When he opened it, César greeted him and then entered the small room. César looked at Steve, nodded, and quickly surveyed the rest of the room before saying *buenas noches* to Steve and the rest. Pépe followed in right behind him.

"*Que tal, camaradas!*" Pépe yelled out to Bernardo and Fernando. And then smiling at Steve, "We meet again, gringo."

"Pépe! You're not in jail?" Steve blurted out, amazed to see him.

"No, not any longer," he grinned. "I did not like the food much. Or the hospitality."

Steve gazed down at Pépe's swollen, bloody hand and at his injured leg still wrapped in the dirty gauze.

"What in the hell happened to your hand?"

"Nothing, amigo. I was attack by wild beast," he said in his broken English. "But I kill the animal."

"So gringo," César said politely. "Fernando and Pépe tell me you wish to speak with me."

"That's right. I would like to interview the *campesinos* who saw the plane crash and the *campesino* killings. I think they're connected.

I'd like to print the truth about what really happened. But I'll need your help to get me an interview with the witnesses."

"You'll print the truth?" César said, more a statement than a question.

"You know that you're being accused of the *campesino* killings, and I know it wasn't possible for you to have been in Machipa at the time the killings took place."

"How is that, gringo?"

"I saw Colonel Montero's report. He has the killings of the *campesinos* at 1:30 in the afternoon. That was around the same time Jennifer and I were with you. And we're both willing to testify to that."

"And the connection you mention?" César asked eyeing him skeptically. "Between the plane and the *campesinos*?"

"Apparently, Montero is deeply involved in both. I'm not sure what he's getting out of this, or who put him up to it. I know he's lying about the slayings, and I believe he's lying about the plane. And I think he silenced the *campesinos* so they would never be able to reveal the truth about the plane. Whatever the truth is."

"And so you, my gringo friend, are willing to testify against the colonel?"

"Yes, if I have the evidence I need to back me."

"And your Embassy friends? What do they believe?"

"I'm not sure what you mean about my Embassy friends. I can't say I have any friends at the Embassy. I do believe if Montero's story works for them, that is, it supports American interests, whatever those interests are, the Embassy will go along with him."

"And what do you think about American interests? You do not wish to support your country's interests, gringo?"

"Not if it means supporting murder."

"So, gringo, you are not without values." He smiled, perhaps more amused than convinced. "Let me drink to that. *Dame*," he said, pointing to the bottle on the table.

Fernando passed the glass and bottle to him.

"To you, friend. A gringo with values. Let's hope there are more like you." He raised the glass in a toast and then downed the beer.

"Fernando, give the bottle to my gringo friend."

"*Gracias*." Steve took the bottle and filled his glass. Then he returned to the subject of Montero.

130

"To prove that the colonel lied, that he lied about the plane and about you and the Machipa *campesinos*, I need your help, your witnesses."

César didn't say a word. Instead, he searched the gringo's eyes for the smallest sign of betrayal. Steve could feel his stare drilling into him. He knew César was no fool, that he needed to believe he could trust him, so he was looking for something to convince him. Steve could be making up the story about Montero's report, though César knew that the Shining Path had already been accused of killing the *campesinos*. It had been all over the news. But César also knew of gringos that did not support the army or the police, or their own government's policies, for that matter. Certainly he knew of Lori Berenson, the *gringa* that had served more than fifteen years in a Peruvian prison because of her involvement with the MRTA, the Túpac Amaru Revolutionary Movement. Her dedication and commitment to their cause had to be legend among the *Senderistas*, although César would've been too young to have known her personally.

No one in the room made a sound. Their eyes were on César, except for Pépe, occupied with an old woman busy cleaning his leg wound. He cringed as he held on to his bloody pants leg. He had it raised above his knee so the woman could douse his leg with alcohol.

"Okay, friend, I will bring you proof tomorrow, the two witnesses. But you come alone. Is that understood?"

"Yes, that's clear," Steve said, sucking in a mouthful of air and then breathing out deeply. It looked like it was going to happen. He'd gotten what he'd come for. "What time?"

"Four in the afternoon."

Back in the bus he leaned his head against the back seat and stared up at the ceiling. For Christ's sake, it must be true, he thought. The massacres and the plane crash. The rebels had nothing to do with either. Why else would César go along with him, agreeing to produce witnesses? And that fucking Montero. He was sure the colonel was an assassin. Everything about Montero creeped him out, from his phony smile to the bullshit charm he turned on whenever Jennifer was under his radar.

So if César did produce witnesses tomorrow, then what? He would meticulously document the meeting. Even get it on video. The one thought that nagged at him was that the bastards responsible for the murders could always question the witnesses' credibility. Why would anyone believe a couple of *campesinos* that César Montalvo produced? A Shining Path leader the CIA had put a five-million-dollar bounty on.

They would believe it because of Montero's report. The colonel had screwed up royally, claiming César committed the genocide at a time when he could not have. Jennifer had his actual fucking report, signed and dated! The colonel was going down. He and Jennifer would testify that his allegation against César was a lie.

He couldn't wait until tomorrow to hear the *campesinos'* account. If their story held together, then he would need to decide whether to see the ambassador first, or take the story directly to the press. He wasn't convinced he could trust Ambassador Wenton. His experience had been that American Embassy officials mistrusted any group with leftist ideas. In fact, most government bureaucrats mistrusted any group or party that questioned free market orthodoxy. Neoliberalism was pretty much the only punch government bureaucrats drank these days. And they were punch drunk. They saw the world one way and one way only. Hell, some of them probably saw Obama as a socialist, Steve reflected. That's how FOX News portrayed him. What a stretch. He was no more a socialist than Bill Clinton, the man whose NAFTA agreement was responsible for weakening the unions and moving US industry overseas.

To be fair, the Shining Path scared the hell out of conservatives and liberals alike. Although Maoism had been a brutal failure, universally discredited and abhorred, the Shining Path wanted to resurrect it. For this reason, Ambassador Wenton would have a hard time accepting the witnesses' credibility. But Jennifer had Montero's report. That was the clincher. The report would reinforce the *campesinos'* story. As long as they had the report, the ambassador could be convinced. And if he believed them, then he would be inclined to investigate the senator's death. To get the real culprits, they would need to discover what happened to Kursten.

But he would have to be careful. Careful but not cowardly. As dangerous as his journalistic meddling might become, he couldn't turn his back and walk away, not after knowing what he knew. Those poor *campesinos* deserved better. Innocent people murdered to cover up a lie. A lie to support a political agenda

Tomorrow they would have the proof they needed, as long as the witnesses cooperated. He couldn't wait to tell Jennifer. They'd finally have the colonel's ass. Then they'd be able go after the real devils! Whatever the cost, they'd find out what the connection was between Senator Kursten and the *campesino* massacre. Nothing was going to stop them now.

20

"Hey, I was expecting to see you last night? What time did you get back?"

Steve had just sat down for breakfast in the hotel dining room when Jennifer walked in and plopped down in a chair across from him.

"Around 10:30. Sorry about not ringing you. I planned on dropping by your room, but after showering I had a couple beers, turned on the TV, and then fell asleep watching a documentary on Discovery."

He was lying really, except about the shower and beers. And felt guilty about it. But the truth was he had needed to be alone. About half way through his second beer, he started thinking that maybe he was making a big mistake dragging her into all of this. He had this feeling that he was staring into a bottomless pit and it was just a matter of time before both of them were sucked in. The alcohol had added to his funk. After his sixth beer, he was in no condition to see anyone.

"Around 11:00, I checked with the receptionist and he said you were in your room. I assumed alone this time," she chuckled. "I figured that you'd be knocking on my door any minute, and then before I knew it, it was one in the morning."

She rested her elbows on the table and her head in her hands, studying him, apparently trying to pick up any clue as to what might be troubling him. He was definitely more reticent than usual, and more subdued.

"Did you see César?"

"Yeah, I saw him. The meeting actually went quite well. I'm supposed to meet with him this afternoon. He said he'd bring the old man and his grandson. It looks like the shit is about to hit the fan real soon. One of my boss's favorite expressions," he smiled.

"And my father's too."

"Oh, really?"

"Yeah. No kidding. He used it all of the time."

"So whaddaya say we celebrate the good news! We break out a bottle later?" She placed her hand over his and squeezed it. "If we have the witnesses' testimony, that should be the nail in the colonel's coffin."

"Yep. Should be," he said, his face clouding over. "You know, last night I was thinking about my life and how things have ended up. Last time I got this deep into anything political it turned out to be a real disaster. I thought about how just one single event in a person's life can totally alter it. I was wondering if it might not be far worse this time. I'm not sure who or what we might be up against. US foreign policy isn't what we see on CNN. Most Americans know little about our nasty little involvement in the internal affairs of other nations. We talk about how we're the greatest nation on earth. Rarely about our motives, or who really directs foreign policy. And nothing about the many coups we've instrumented. Or our complicity in murder."

His last comment caused her to squirm in her seat.

"Ask the average American college graduate about Arbenz, the president of Guatemala in the early '50s. You'll get zero. But ask the average educated Peruvian, or Latin American, and it wouldn't surprise me if half of them gave you a full history. When Arbenz started screwing with the United Fruit Company, part of his agrarian reform, Eisenhower ordered the CIA to sponsor a coup d'état, code-named Operation PBSUCCESS. That took care of Arbenz. Few Americans know about this sad event. It's an inconvenient truth. Around the same time, on the other side of the world, President Mosaddegh wanted to nationalize his country's oil. Another US sponsored coup occurred, led by the illustrious Kermit Roosevelt, the grandson of President Theodore Roosevelt. The same shit continued into the sixties and seventies. Declassified documents show that the CIA received directions to 'liquidate' President Sukarno."

"Liquidate?"

"Yeah, that's the word that was used."

"He must have made some serious enemies in Washington."

"Yeah, I'd say. Perhaps the classic example of unlawful US intervention is Chile and Allende in '73. The CIA was behind the attack on the government palace, and maybe his murder. And Allende was the democratically elected president of Chile. ITT put up millions, along with Anaconda Copper, to defeat him in the presidential elections, and when this didn't work, more extreme measures were chosen. Allende wanted socialism, wanted to nationalize key industries, wanted agrarian reform. Wanted to enact a host of policies not good for foreign investment. Or not good for the kind of foreign investment third world countries are accustomed to.

"Argentina, Uruguay, Brazil—all military coups supported by our government. You know, thousands of innocent people were disappeared in Argentina and Chile, but that was all fine and dandy as long as their misery and death resulted in a favorable business climate. The same is true about Gadafi. When he made it too tough for foreign oil companies, he had to go. Not that the sicko ever had my sympathy. I'll never forget what happened to the 270 people aboard Pan Am Flight 107, many of them students."

"Yeah, that was horrible. I remember watching a program about it on TV. I was only a kid."

"It's mostly about money, Jennifer. Money and power. That's what it's always been about. But you know," he said, his eyes trained on hers, "instead of this depressing the shit out of me, this morning when I woke up, I convinced myself that none of it should put a damper on what we need to do. We could just throw in the towel and say fuck it, We're up against something we can't defeat. Maybe that would be the sane thing to do. Are you sure you want to get involved in something so dangerous?"

"I'm sure," she said, still holding his hand.

"You know, Jennifer, when I think of what happened in Machipa, it makes me sick. What do our lives mean, if we can turn away, shrug our shoulders, and say, 'Sorry, not much we can do'? No, if I can make it happen, those who are responsible will pay."

"You make me so proud."

And he knew that she meant it. He could see it in her eyes. Her cheeks had turned chrisom and her voice had a faint strain.

"Yeah, we have a chance to be the good guys," she smiled nervously. "So, let's just do what's right and let the axe fall where it may."

"You are one beautiful woman, Jennifer. And it appears every bit as naive as I am! I love it!" He reached across the table and touched her cheek. "It feels great to be doing the right thing with the right woman. I couldn't be happier."

"You know, I'm really going to miss you when this is all over. I've really enjoyed myself the last few days, despite the danger."

"Hey, it's a bit early for goodbyes. And I hope when the time comes, it's just a short one."

"It will be. I promise you. I believe that this is just the beginning of something wonderful. Geez," she said, suddenly animated. "We're acting like our work is all done and it's really only starting. Speaking of which, when's your interview with the *campesinos*? And what was it like last night? Were you scared? Were there many of César's men with him?"

"One question at a time," he laughed.

"Sorry," she said, puckering her lips into a pout.

"Yes, I was scared."

"How many of César's men were there?"

"Just a few. I'm supposed to meet him around four at the same place. Hey, by the way, Pépe broke out of jail! He was there with César!"

"Wow! No kidding. Good for him! I guess. God, I'm sounding like a rebel sympathizer! So that's what the noise and sirens were about last night. It sounded like a shoot-out at the O. K. Corral."

"Was it that bad? Were you frightened?"

"A little. But I stayed in the hotel. I heard a couple of explosions, one very far away and the other very close to the hotel. And then a bunch of shooting. It lasted maybe about ten minutes, but seemed a lot longer."

Then suddenly changing the subject, "Hey, do you want me to tag along when you meet with César?"

"Afraid not. I promised him I would come alone. He still doesn't trust me a whole lot."

Jennifer rose and stepped around the table and held out her arms motioning him to come over to her.

Steve stood up admiring her for a few seconds before pulling her into him and folding his arms around her and feeling her slender body pressed against his. He gave her a solid squeeze, wishing that he could hold onto her forever.

She leaned her face against his chest momentarily and then suddenly raised her head and looked at him with a strange sadness in her eyes that he had not seen before. Then with a smile frayed along the edges she said, "Look partner, don't do anything foolish. No heroics, okay? Just get the interview and then high tail it back to Dodge. I'll see you when you return."

When she finished her last sentence, she broke away from him, but too quickly, almost like she was fleeing something or somebody. He sensed something was wrong, but he'd have to leave it until he returned. Women. Hard creatures to figure out, he mused. No matter how much time you spend around them, or how well you think you know them, there is always this hidden part of them that remains a mystery.

* * *

Jennifer took Montero's manila envelope from the top of the dresser and withdrew the report on the Machipa massacre. After today, her mission would be complete. Montalvo would be captured, and the Shining Path's operations in the Huallaga Valley would be severely weakened. The CIA, working with the Peruvian Army, would make sure the Maoist rebels never again posed a threat like they had in the 90s.

So, she had done her part, she reflected, as she held the report in her hand and set the envelope back on the dresser. US foreign policy could not get bogged down because someone got hurt. She had to consider the loss of innocent lives as collateral damage. Sad, but unavoidable.

But forty-three innocent *campesinos* caught in the crossfire. Many of them women and children. No, sad wasn't the word for what had occurred in Machipa. Or collateral damage a simple justification. Lives were not things. Her head of operations had told her Machipa didn't concern them. Her mission had been to help defeat a leftist insurgency that threatened to tear to shreds Peru's delicate fabric of democracy. Did she really think that her job would be easy? That there wouldn't be innocent victims? She had wanted field work, so she got field work. Now she'd just have to accept what came with it.

And Steve? He was also a part of what came with it. She cringed over the thought of how he would take it when he learned of her betrayal. He never saw it coming. Not for a second. Steve at heart was a dreamer. His feet were not planted firmly in the real world. In time he would get over her. But would she get over him? Their relationship had gone farther than it should have, and her heart would have to pay the price.

Jennifer carried the report into the bathroom, opened the door of the medicine cabinet, and removed a box of matches. After staring at the report for several seconds, she struck a match and lit the bottom of the page. She studied the orange flame crawling up its edges as she dangled the paper over the toilet bowl, watching it blacken and shrivel. As soon as she felt the flame begin to lick her finger tips, she released what was left of the report. For a few moments she gazed at the black flakes lying on the surface of the water. Then she pulled the lever and watched as they eddied round and round before being sucked down into oblivion.

She stepped over to the sink, turned on the faucet and began scrubbing her hands to remove any taint of smoke. As she dried her hands, she glanced up at her face in the mirror. In her own mind, she looked older, her youth and enthusiasm replaced by something hard to describe, but whatever she saw momentarily sent a cold shudder through her.

She bent over the sink and filled her cupped hands with water and splashed her face. Then she pressed her fingers against her eyelids, rubbing them, trying to relieve the tension that had collected there. She straightened up and grabbed the towel off the rack and began padding her face with it, intentionally avoiding the mirror.

Yes, she had accomplished her mission all right. But like some foolish young soldier just out of boot camp, attracted to the glamour and honor of serving her country, had not calculated the cost to others. To those caught in between.

For the first time, she was having serious second thoughts about her career. Colombia hadn't prepared her for Peru. In Bogota, she'd interviewed several members of the FARC, but had spent no time in the field. Back then, she had no idea what day to day survival meant for the desperately poor. She knew nothing about their simple dreams. Their basic needs. She'd never seen their lives up close. Never visited a rebel camp and had a real conversation with a rebel leader.

Her belief about America's role in the world was unshakeable then. She had imagined guerillas as a bunch of mad, bearded radicals. Che Guevara types, looking as much like Charles Manson as Che. Their only aim, to tear down everything good and decent.

In César's camp what she actually saw was an armed insurgency of poor farmers. *Campesinos* fighting for a better life, while surviving on the bare minimum. They weren't madmen. If anything, their goals were clear and well-defined. César struck her as a brave, defiant leader committed to social change. With the wrong ideas on how to bring change about, but nonetheless committed. Most of his men could care less about abstruse economic theories, about free markets and trickledown economics. The truth was they didn't give a good damn about economic fundamentals. All they knew was that they were dirt poor and nothing was trickling down to them.

She glanced in the mirror again and noticed how tired her face looked. In college, she thought she had a solid grasp on politics and economics. Maybe she did. Maybe, in Peru, she had gotten too close to the action and couldn't see the forest because of the trees. Couldn't see the larger picture. Just the human misery. Regardless of the simple, honest beliefs of the Peruvian poor, communism would be far worse for them. US policy and free market economics had created a better living standard for the poor worldwide. The stats were there. And in places where free market economics seemed to have failed, it was because of the corrupt officials who mismanaged government or stole from the public coffers.

Or, had she been brainwashed into believing something that wasn't true? Steve had definitely planted doubt in her with his left of center ideas. But was it really his ideas that had a grip on her, or her feelings about him?

If Steve was right, then who were the bad guys? Certainly not César or Pépe. In his mind, they were just simple folks ready and willing to lay down their lives for the dream of a better world for themselves and their children. Not bad guys at all.

But for her, they had chosen the wrong means, the wrong political philosophy. Wanton violence was never the answer.

And the forty-three *campesinos* that the butcher Montero had murdered? Yes, no doubt they'd been caught in between. But in between what, exactly? Congressman Kursten was still a mystery. In the case of Colonel Montero, she had no problem identifying the bad guy. She had the facts. What bothered her was that having the facts didn't seem to matter. The bad guy would go free, and, for political reasons, she had chosen to protect him.

But goddamn it! She had to believe that in the larger view US policy is correct. We can't control the likes of all the Monteros in the world. Every country has crazy, ruthless bastards like him.

She opened her purse and reached tentatively for her cell phone. Her hand was shaking as she punched in the numbers.

"Mr. Pierce, please."

It took only a few seconds for him to answer.

"Hello, any news? Has your Mister Collins arranged to meet Montalvo?"

Your Mister Collins? She didn't particularly like his tone. It sounded condescending, like Steve was just an object. Her Mr. Collins, to be used as she wished.

"He's getting ready to leave the hotel now. He'll be meeting Montalvo in the afternoon at around 16:00. *Manzana C, Lote 2*, San Ramon."

"Any idea on numbers?"

"Most likely a half a dozen rebels."

"Did he say where?"

"No."

"Okay, we'll take it from there."

The next thing she heard was a click and then a low static buzz. She held the phone to her ear listening to the humming sound, to the finality of her irrevocable message. The choice had been hers. Now she would have to live with it.

She dialed the desk. *"Aló?* This is Jennifer Strand in room 204. I'll need a taxi for the airport at around 3:30."

"Si, *Señorita.*"

21

While Steve was leaving the hotel to catch a bus for his rendezvous with César, a young soldier crossed the street and asked him for identification documents. Steve removed his passport and his SPJ card from his shirt pocket. As the soldier examined his docs, a military jeep sped over to the curb and squealed to a stop. Colonel Montero got out.

"*Buenas tardes*, Mr. Collins." The Colonel turned to the soldier and ordered him to return Steve's documents. The soldier immediately handed Steve his passport and journalist card, saluted the colonel, and then stepped away.

"It's procedure to ask for documents, especially after last night. You heard about last night?"

"Yeah, I caught something in the paper about an attack on two police stations."

"Yes. The terrorists attacked two police headquarters. One attack was apparently a diversion. The other one was on the headquarters where Pépe Canchari was being held. You know Canchari. You and Miss Strand interviewed him the day before yesterday."

"Oh, yes. And Canchari?"

"He's gone. They managed to break him out. Some policemen were killed in both attacks."

"I'm sorry to hear that, Colonel."

"Well, if we find the bastard Canchari, next time his friends won't be able to free him from jail," he said studying Steve's face. "But he's probably faraway from here by now, hiding out with his commie bastards."

The colonel slid his sun glasses up on his nose. "You have a good day, *Señor* Collins. Sorry about the soldier detaining you."

"No problem." Steve turned and walked in the direction of the bus stop on the other side of the plaza.

As he crossed the street, a little Indian girl in faded red shorts and a soiled light green pullover stepped out of the alley holding a scrawny kitten. Steve noticed MRTA painted in broad red letters on the wall behind her. The letters stood for *Movimiento Revolucionario Tupac Amaru*, or in English, Tupac Amaru Revolutionary Movement. Tupac Amaru, a 16th century revolutionary hero, had fought against the Spanish before he was captured and beheaded. That was one story. Another version had it he was drawn and quartered. In any event, not a pleasant ending for the rebel. Painted beside the letters were the ubiquitous hammer and sickle.

The little girl looked up at Steve and snuggled her cat against the side of her face. He stopped suddenly and withdrew a ten *soles* note from his pocket and handed it to her. A bill equivalent to roughly three American dollars. The little girl held the money in her small hand looking as though she had just inherited a fortune. She glanced up at him with a shy smile, cocking her head to the side to get a better look at the gringo who had appeared out of nowhere. Scrunched up in her hand was more money than her parents, assuming she had parents, made in an entire day. Steve stopped, smiled back at her, and told her not to lose the money. "*Guardalo bien*," he said, and then darted across the street.

It took Steve about an hour to get from the *Plaza de Armas* to the poor district of town where he was to meet César. The day had started out clear but soon a thick layer of low-hanging clouds darkened the sky. The afternoon showers had been light at first, but now heavy rain fisted the earth. Water gushed down the streets from the hills above, threatening to overflow the shallow gutters. Peering outside the bus window through the tenebrous curtain of rain, he had difficulty making out the buildings and street signs.

Steve worked his way toward the front of the bus and asked the bus driver to drop him off at the Repsol service station near the top of the hill on *Calle Valencia*. He remembered the gas station at the turn off to Fernando's street.

Twenty minutes later, Steve stood in front of Fernando's house. He'd brought along a folder with a few blank sheets of paper inside, and in his jacket pocket he'd tucked away a small digital camera that would allow him to record fifteen minutes or so of video. Before he could knock, the door opened and Pépe's grinning face appeared as he motioned Steve to come in.

"*Buenas tardes*, my friend. Enter. We have been waiting for you," Pépe blurted out warmly, pleased to see him.

Once Steve was inside the house, Pépe poked his head back through the door and gazed down the street in the direction of the service station where Steve had disembarked from the bus. Steve glanced around the room and noticed César seated at the table to the right with a *campesino*, an old man in his seventies. His dark skin highlighted his silvery white hair, giving him a sort of grandfatherly dignity. He'd placed his straw hat on the table and was nervously rubbing its brim, squeezing its edge between his boney thumb and forefinger.

In the two chairs to the left of the old man sat a young *campesino*. At first, he would not look directly at Steve, but kept his head bowed while gazing on his hands resting on the table. When he finally glanced up, he did so timidly with an edgy distrust.

"Hello gringo," César said, and then gestured toward the old man seated at the table. "Here are your witnesses. Juan Pablo saw Montero's men murder his people near his village. He and his grandson heard shots in the distance when they were returning to the village from a visit to their uncle's in Huanuco. They hid in the jungle and saw everything."

Then turning to the old man he told him that the gringo was an American journalist, that his name was Mr. Collins, and he wanted to hear about the soldiers.

The old man extended his dark, sun-baked hand to Steve. Steve felt the old man's thin hand close around his in a weak, timid handshake.

"It's a pleasure sir," Steve said smiling at the old man, hoping to put him at ease.

César turned to the young man. "Armando, Mr. Collins would like to talk to you about the plane crash and the killings you and your grandfather witnessed."

"It is a pleasure to meet you *señor*," the young *campesino* said smiling shyly.

"It's my pleasure," Steve replied, shaking the young *campesino's* hand.

Down the hill two blocks from Fernando's house a white delivery van pulled over to the side of the road. The rain had picked up again, pelting the truck, the raindrops dancing wildly across its roof and hood. The truck's cab door flew open and the driver jumped down and hurried around to the back of the truck. He slid the tailgate upwards and twenty soldiers jumped out. At the same time, Colonel Montero climbed out of the cab and scuttled toward the back of the truck to join his men. As soon as he appeared, they forgot about the rain, straightened up, and put their hands to their sides against their pants leg. The colonel said a few words to the young lieutenant standing next to him and then pointed up the hillside in the direction of Fernando's house. The lieutenant motioned for half of the soldiers to circle around behind the house, and for the other half to follow him and the colonel.

Steve, seated across from the old man, took the legal pad from the folder he had stuffed in his jacket and set it on the table in front of him. Then he removed his camera from his jacket pocket, placed it next to the legal pad, and pushed the record button.

Pépe, resting in one of the chairs against the wall, was absorbed in *El Condorito*, a popular comic book, while César leaned back in his chair underneath a cheap plaster crucifix listening closely to the conversation between Steve and the old man.

"César told me that you saw the killings that happened at your village," Steve began.

"Yes, I saw them," he said. He did not look directly at Steve, but instead concentrated his thoughts on the grainy table top.

"And would you tell me what you saw?" Steve asked, at the same time realizing how difficult this was going to be for the old guy.

"The soldiers," he began again slowly, painfully drawing the words out, "they had everyone gather together outside of town. They'd brought them from our village. We were hiding, watching them, my grandson and me. We had just returned from Huanaco. The soldiers pushed them, poking them with their rifles and then made them all get down on their knees at the side of the road. Several of the women began crying. Little Patti, my great granddaughter, got frightened and broke loose from her mother and started running back toward the village. A soldier grabbed her before she could get very far and pushed her down next to her mother, my granddaughter. Her mother grabbed her. Little Patti was crying, *señor*, while her mother held her, patting her hair, telling her not to worry. That God would protect them. But *señor*, my granddaughter was crying herself. It was terrible *señor*, terrible. My whole village was there, kneeling by the side of the road. Most of them were praying, asking the Virgin Mother to help them. More than a dozen soldiers stood behind them with their rifles pointed at their backs, waiting for the colonel to give the order."

Here the old man paused, having great difficulty continuing. Steve could tell that he was trying his best to get the words out, but they seemed to have stuck in his windpipe. Finally, after a few moments had passed, he cleared his throat and picked up where he had left off.

"The colonel, he stepped to the side. Then he nodded his head to his officer. The officer then gave the order for the rest of the soldiers to fire."

"At everyone? The women and children too?" Steve asked almost in disbelief.

"Si *Señor*, everyone. Women and children. Everyone. My son and his wife, my niece, my sister, her husband, my granddaughter, and Little Patti, everyone, *señor*."

The old man raised his fingers to his eyes attempting to push back the tears that had gathered in the corners.

"I'm so sorry." Steve didn't know what else to say. No words could stop the hurt inside the old man. He could only try to imagine what he'd felt, and was now feeling. His children, his family, and his friends executed before his very eyes. He and his grandson unable to do anything. Sitting there in the brush horrified and helpless.

He wished there was another way to obtain the information he needed. Asking this old man to recall such a horrific scene, just didn't seem right. He felt ashamed asking him to recount such dreadful moments, though he knew there was no other way.

Armando had placed his hand on his grandfather's, trying to comfort him, though his own eyes had welled up with tears. Steve changed the subject, addressing the grandson.

"César tells me that you also saw the plane crash. And that you saw a man jump out of the plane right before it crashed. Could you tell me what you remember?"

"Si *Señor*, I saw a man fall from the plane and a parachute open. Right before the plane began to drop from the sky. This is what I told the people in our village. In town some of them spread the word the Shining Path did not shoot down the plane. That the military was lying. The people said my grandfather and I saw the plane crash. I believe the colonel came to my village asking for me and my grandfather, but we had gone to visit my uncle in Huanuco. He was very sick. Before we left to go to my uncle's home in Huanaco, we heard that the colonel had been asking about us. We are alive only because we were not in the village when he came."

"You said that a man parachuted from the plane."

"Si *Señor*. I went with my dog Kiki to look for the man so I could help him if he was hurt. I did not find him. It was when we were returning to our village, Kiki started sniffing around in the bushes and barking. I went over to see what he had found. He had dug a hole where the man buried his parachute."

"Buried his parachute?"

"Si *Señor*. And when we looked at the parachute, I saw large black letters that said, US ARMY and some other word I don't know. I put the parachute under my bed. It is still there, unless the soldiers have found it and taken it."

"Before you found the parachute, did you get to the place where the plane crashed?"

"Si *Señor*. We saw the plane. It had only part of a wing. Pieces of the plane were scattered in the field. Not just plane parts, *señor*, but parts of people, *señor*."

He looked ill as he recalled the grisly scene. His eyes were no longer teared up, but instead large and filled with terror.

"I remember seeing the burnt body of a soldier and a man dressed in a business suit. Parts of them, I mean. The pilot was smashed in with the front part of the plane where the instruments are. Most of the body was there, still strapped into the seat, but the head, *señor*, was not there. Just the lower part of the body. We also saw an arm in the grass outside the plane. It was the arm of the man with the business suit."

"Would you be willing to tell your story to officials at the American Embassy? If I can get the embassy to guarantee no one will hurt you or your family?"

Armando looked at César waiting for César to say something. César broke the awkward moment of silence, addressing Steve in English.

"And gringo, do you really think the word of your government is worth risking this family's life? They have seen firsthand how the government here works."

"I promise to have a written commitment from the US Embassy to protect them. The officials at the Embassy will need to take the witnesses' statements. If I don't have the Embassy's guarantee first, then I won't ask them to come forward and testify. I do know this, if he and his grandfather say nothing, there will be no justice for his family and friends. And he and his grandfather will be forced to live from now on in fear of being captured by the colonel's men."

"Do you know what the military does to informers?" César asked, his eyes locked on Steve's.

"I can get a commitment from the Embassy not to disclose information about them. And even if the Peruvian authorities were to somehow discover their identities, they would be foolish to lay their hands on them, if my own government asks for immunity."

Steve then turned back to the *campesino* and his grandfather. "If you are willing to tell my government what you saw, I will get my government to promise to protect you. I believe you will be safe. If you cooperate, you'll have a chance to bring to justice those who murdered your family and friends."

The grandson would not look at him, or the grandfather. Both had their heads bowed. Pépe stood across from them rubbing his battered knuckles.

"I can only give you my word," Steve said as he stood up from the table, picked up his camera, turned off the video recorder, and stuck it in his jacket pocket.

César was just about to say something when the door burst open and three soldiers with automatic weapons poised to fire stepped into the room.

"*No se muevan, carajo!*" one of them shouted.

Seconds later the colonel himself stepped into the room.

César made a move to go for his hand gun, but the soldiers raised their weapons at the same time and aimed them directly at his face. Then one of the soldiers, an officer, approached him and punched him in the rib with the butt of his weapon. César collapsed on the floor and drew his knees into his chest. The officer kicked him in the side and then placed his foot on his face and told him to be still. He kicked the gun out of César's waistband and watched it sail across the floor. The colonel told one of soldiers to pick up the gun and bring it to him.

The colonel took the gun and bent down to where César lay on the floor holding his side. Placing the gun against his temple, he ordered him to get up from the floor.

He slowly rose, holding his side, all the time his eyes fixed in a cold hard stare on Steve.

"So, now gringo, we see what your word is really worth," he said and then spat on the floor.

Steve looked at the colonel in utter disbelief and then at Pépe who shared César's disgust.

"*Gracias,* Mr. Collins. *Manzana C, Lote 2,* very clear directions," Colonel Montero said turning to Steve. "My government appreciates your help."

A paralyzing chill shot up Steve's spine as it suddenly dawned on him what had happened. How else would the colonel have known Fernando's address? No! It was too incredible to be true! But how then? Jennifer? No, the idea was unthinkable. The colonel's men must have followed him. Yes, that was it! That had to be it! But his half numb brain was telling him differently.

In a daze, he watched the colonel and his soldiers shove the old man, the nephew, Pépe, César, and the others outside. The whole area around the house was completely surrounded by soldiers.

Totally stunned, he stared at the colonel's men as they herded César and his bunch into the back of a military truck. The soldiers couldn't have just followed him, he realized. There were too many of them and the operation was too organized. This had all been planned.

"I trust you'll find a way back to the hotel," the colonel said, hurrying off toward the front of the truck to escape the rain. "Give my regards to *Senorita* Strand!" he yelled out, and then climbed into the cab slamming the door shut.

The driver threw the truck into gear and Steve watched as it lurched forward down the hill, the other truck with the prisoners following right behind it.

Unable to focus his thoughts, he stood as still as a corpse in the middle of the street staring at the muddy tire tracks and the deep ruts left by the two trucks.

The streets were completely empty. No one had dared to venture outside, but it seemed everywhere he looked frightened, dark faces filled the windows.

He would never forget how Pépe and César's expressions fixed on him when the soldiers burst into the house. There was only one way he could describe what he saw in their eyes. Pure loathing.

"Give my regards to Senorita Strand!" The colonel's words echoed in his head as he fought to piece together details about Jennifer. He started with the first night they met. Had it all been a set up? Meeting her at the dance hall in Rimac? And her suggestion—not his—that they "get some fresh air"? Then accidently bumping into her the next day at the office of *The Lima Tribune*. Was it possible she'd planned it all from the very beginning? No way! There had to be some other explanation.

To escape the rain, he began jogging down the hill to the small store on the corner where the bus had dropped him. By the time he reached the store, he was drenched. Near the entrance, he saw a public telephone. He hurried inside and asked the man behind the counter for change. Reaching into his rear pocket, he took out his wallet and removed a card from the Esperanza hotel.

He rushed outside, deposited a coin in the payphone, and dialed the hotel. "Please have it not be true," he told himself as he listened to the rain pattering against the tin awning above him.

"*Aló*, Hotel Esperanza," the desk clerk answered.

"Look, this is Mr. Collins. I need to speak to Ms. Strand. Could you get her for me?"

"I'm sorry Mr. Collins. Ms. Strand checked out of the hotel about two hours ago, shortly after you left. She asked me to call a cab for her, to take her to the airport."

Steve's heart sank as he set the phone back in its cradle. So, it was true. He'd been played. Ms. Jennifer Strand—it was doubtful that was her real name—had played him and played him well. Like a pro. She'd gotten what she'd come for. César Montalvo.

And him? The naïve, dumbshit journalist? Well, he was just collateral damage. Like the *campesinos* of Machipa. Alive, but inside feeling just as dead.

22

As soon as Steve settled into the chair, he began rubbing his knees to get his blood circulating. It was an unusually hot day in Lima, but inside the conference room it was freezing.

He was not sure where to start or how Ambassador Wenton would digest what he was about to tell him. More than likely, Wenton had been privy to the CIA's machinations to use him to capture Montalvo.

He had one thing going for him. He'd learned from his boss at *The Lima Tribune* that John Brinton had been a friend of Senator Kursten. Any suggestion of a connection between the Machipa massacre and the senator's death, Brinton would surely want to hear about.

Steve's stomach was burning like he had just swallowed battery acid. The Pepto-Bismol he'd taken at his apartment wasn't working. He had to try to control his emotions, forget about how he'd been screwed over by Strand. He'd begin with the *campesino* killings and the cover-up involving the crash. He'd leave Jennifer Strand for later. But keeping quiet about her was easier said than done. Her treachery had delivered more of a blow to his heart than to his ego. As angry as he was about being used by her, he couldn't deny that fact. But now she was out of here. Mission accomplished. It was that goddamn simple.

Steve spoke non-stop for five minutes filling in Ambassador Wenton and John Brinton about the interview with the old man and his grandson. He started with their account of what had happened to the plane. They sat absorbing every detail, not once interrupting him. When Steve finished neither of them said a word. Finally, the ambassador broke the silence by telling him he didn't know what to make of the *campesino's* story. Especially the part about a man jumping from the plane before it crashed. He confided that he had pretty much accepted Montero's report, that the plane had been struck by a missile fired by the Shining Path.

Steve could see that neither of them had been convinced that the plane had simply lost power and plummeted to the earth. He knew that both of them needed more convincing.

Suddenly he remembered an important detail he'd left out. What Armando had told him about finding a parachute with US ARMY stamped on it. He decided to tell them about it, but not mention that Armando had hidden the parachute in his house under the bed. That might not be wise.

After hearing him out, they still didn't appear convinced. Their unresponsiveness troubled him. Maybe he'd been wrong to approach them and believe he could win their trust. Then again, maybe he was being too paranoid and judgmental. He understood that there was no love between him and embassy folk. His prejudice could be clouding his opinion of them. It could be that they just needed to weigh everything carefully before responding.

Well, it was time to find out. He'd tell them about Montero and Machipa. And if that didn't convince them of a connection between Machipa and the congressman's death, then he'd be at the end of his road. Where he'd go from there, he had no idea. Help from the *campesinos* was not an option any more. He was certainly on their shit list. And the old man and his grandson? Montero would be sure to silence them.

When he started telling him about the old man and his grandson witnessing the Machipa murders, he had them riveted. But then when he broke it to them that the two *campesinos* had actually witnessed Colonel Montero giving the order to kill the villagers, Wenton and Brinton both looked at him curiously, like a shrink would look at one of his patients, all sympathy and understanding, but zero credibility.

"So you're saying the same two *campesinos* that saw the plane crash saw Colonel Montero give the orders to kill the villagers. Is that what you're saying?" Wenton asked.

"Yes, that's what I'm saying. They saw Colonel Montero give the order to his officer. And they did not mistake the colonel for someone else. No one in or around Tingo María would mistake the colonel because they all hate his fucking guts. You'll have to excuse my French, gentleman."

"If they hate him, as you say they do, that would certainly be a good reason to frame him. Also, you only have their testimony. Under ordinary circumstances, two eye witnesses would be enough to call for an investigation into the murders, but then there is another problem."

"And what might that be?" Steve knew full well where the ambassador was headed. Raise doubt about the evidence by attacking the credibility of the witnesses.

"They are not just your ordinary *campesinos*, Mr. Collins. If I understand you correctly, they were both arrested by the Peruvian military at the same time as César Montalvo, which raises a serious

152

question about why they were with him. It could very well be that they are terrorists themselves."

"I hope you don't really believe that. It sounds like a claim the colonel himself would make. Just because they were arrested with Montalvo, does not make them Shining Path. No more than it makes me a member of the Shining Path. You need to remember, I was there when they were arrested, and they were there because I had asked for an interview and arranged the interview with Montalvo."

"Well quite frankly, Mr. Collins, it does sound like you were a bit chummy with Montalvo yourself. I mean a personal interview with a Shining Path leader, how did your pull that off?" John Brinton asked.

There it was, the fucking brainwashing, the wall that he suspected he'd be butting his head against. Any journalist associating with a terrorist had to be a commie himself, or at best a commie sympathizer.

"Well, it's like this Mr. Brinton. I guess you can believe what you want. And no, I wasn't chummy with him. In fact, I almost cashed in my chips trying to get the interview. An interview I discovered too late was more for Ms. Strand than for me."

Shit, there it was. The pent up anger. The damn had sprung a leak. He had to control himself, or else his emotions would dynamite his purpose.

"I'm just asking you both to listen to what the two witnesses have to say, look at the evidence, and then make your own decision. I know what I'm going to do with their testimonies. As a journalist, I have a duty to tell the truth."

With the little evidence he had, or that he had presented to them so far, this was a feeble threat more than anything else, so he wasn't sure how his comment would play out.

As he studied their faces, he could see that his threat had no effect. They simply ignored his remark. Not even an eyebrow twitch.

"This business about the parachute having US ARMY printed on it," the ambassador broke in. "Did you see the parachute?"

So, the parachute had grabbed the Ambassador's attention.

"No, but..." and here Steve wasn't sure where to go next. He could tell them that the parachute might still be in Armando's house, under his bed, but the whereabouts of the parachute was his trump card. He needed to get to the parachute himself. It would be a solid piece of evidence to back the *campesinos'* testimonies. He felt sweat gathering in his armpits, while the chill in the room caused goose bumps to run up and down his arms.

"No, but what?" John Brinton asked. This was only the second time he had spoken.

Quickly an idea came to Steve.

"Armando told me that he gave the parachute to a friend to keep for him. It's in safe keeping."

"Well, if his friend has the parachute, that certainly might be important, though the State Department has now taken over the investigation of the crash," the ambassador added. "Do you think you can get the parachute?"

"I will need to speak to Armando. I doubt that he would tell you anything. He's too scared. I'm not even sure how far I can get with him. Do you know where they are holding him? And can you get permission for me to see him?"

Almost as important to Steve as the parachute was seeing Armando. He needed to explain to him how he had been set up and assure him that he would do all he could to get him released.

"Let me see," the ambassador replied. "Mr. Brinton, please ask Ms. Clark to call General Torres. Tell Margaret to ask the general if he can get one of our people in to see the *campesino*, Armando…What is his last name?" the ambassador asked turning to Steve.

"I don't know. Only first names were used during the interview."

"Mr. Brinton, just ask her to tell the general that we would like to send one of our people over to talk to Armando, the young *campesino* who was arrested with César Montalvo."

"Yes sir, Mr. Ambassador," Brinton said as he slipped out of the conference door.

"I don't know if you know this, but General Torres's nephew was the pilot on the plane. I'm not sure we'll have access to the prisoners. General Torres was quite upset about the crash, to say the least. I saw him a few nights ago at the dinner party we threw at my residence. He wasn't looking so good. He retired a few years ago but has a lot of influence."

"Mr. Ambassador, for what it is worth, I believe the story that the old man and his grandson Armando told me about the killings and about the crash. It was terribly difficult for them to even talk about what happened. The old man could hardly speak about the killings. When I met them, they were scared of being discovered. Armando mentioned that they had to stay in hiding because the colonel wanted them dead. When I suggested that our Embassy would protect them by not revealing their identities if they helped us, I think they would have agreed to come forward, even though they thought they might be risking their own lives. Although they were frightened of what might happen to them, they wanted justice for their families and friends. I'm sure of that."

John Brinton opened the door and stepped back into the conference room. "Margaret said she'd get right back to us once she got through to the general."

"Thanks, Mr. Brinton." And then turning back to Steve, "I will get in touch with you Mr. Collins as soon as I hear from the general. Please leave a number where my secretary can reach you. I assume you have a mobile phone?"

"Yes, Mr. Ambassador."

"Please, leave your mobile number with my secretary. I will do what I can to follow up on the information that you've given us."

"One last thing, Mr. Ambassador. I feel I need to tell you that I did not appreciate being used to get to César Montalvo. And now that I have been, my life is in jeopardy. I'm sure it's out that I betrayed César Montalvo and set up his capture. Did anyone here at the Embassy really think about that? That your covert operation to catch a rebel leader would place in grave danger an American citizen? And that this was all done without his knowledge? All done to assist one of your agents catch César Montalvo."

Now that he had said it, he felt he could breathe a little easier, though he knew that criticizing the Embassy was probably the wrong move if he expected any help from them.

"Between us, Mr. Collins, I had no specific knowledge that you were being used, as you say. The operation to capture César Montalvo was outside of my diplomatic duties as ambassador. Intelligence operations are undertaken by the State Department's intelligence services, which include, as you're probably aware, the DIA, CIA, NSA, and their likes. I generally have little knowledge of their plans and who their plans include. I did not know that Miss Strand was working with anyone in our intelligence services. Mr. Henkly told me she was an embedded journalist and wanted to cover the plane crash. That she had been cleared. That is basically all I knew about her."

Then apologetically, "I'm sorry that you were involved in any of this, and I can imagine how you must feel."

"If you'll indulge me gentlemen, just one question. Why in the hell do we involve ourselves in the internal politics of a sovereign nation? You know as well as I that Miss Strand's business here had nothing to do with our own national security. The Shining Path poses no direct threat to us. There are so many other ways we could help this poor nation and win the goodwill of its people."

"Mr. Collins, let me answer you by saying that I believe firmly that there are national interests that our government needs to address, and it's not my job to meddle in matters that I have only a limited knowledge of. I guess I would say that it's a matter of placing faith and trust in your government. And I understand that not all Americans are willing to do this. But you see Mr. Collins, I am. So I'm not in a position to question CIA operations, if that is in fact what Miss Strand was engaged in."

"I'm sorry to hear that Mr. Ambassador. I personally feel there is a moral structure, for lack of a better word, that no government has the right to violate, and when its 'laws' are violated it is our duty to do the right thing, regardless of our national security, which I personally believe becomes an excuse to support policies that have little to do with national security and a lot to do with business. And I don't mean business on a small scale. No I'm talking about on a large invasive scale, as the myriad of corporate lobbyists in Washington give evidence of."

"But Mr. Collins, certainly you understand that…"

"Please, humor me for a second. I think I deserve that much, though I'm sure there is nothing I can say or do that will get you to see things differently than you see them. What I do know is that the real victims of our foreign policy are easily forgotten, and we leave it to someone else to clean up the mess when things get out of hand. Well, there is one thing that I do promise you. If the terrorists do not get to me first for betraying one of their own, I will do my best to see that the *campesinos* who were murdered get the justice they deserve, and Senator Kursten as well. I'm not one to hang laurels on our politicians, but from what I know of the late senator, he was a pretty good man."

"Well, Mr. Collins, I'm sure that there are a number of issues that we would never agree on, but I respect your honesty and graciously accept any help you can give us. Once I hear back from the general, I will be in touch." Ambassador Wenton extended his hand.

Steve looked at the ambassador's hand, and for a moment thought about refusing to shake it and just simply leaving. However, the ambassador struck him as sincere. Not that Steve liked the straight patriotic line he had drawn in the sand regarding his responsibility to his government, but he sensed the ambassador's compassion and understanding for the *campesino*s, and also for the predicament in which Steve had been placed.

"I look forward to hearing from you Mr. Ambassador," Steve said, taking the ambassador's hand and giving it a firm shake.

As he left the American Embassy, a young woman with a small child tagging along came up to him holding her hand out and asking for money. He glanced at her and then looked away with a pained expression in his eyes.

Then without thinking, he reached into his front pocket and removed a wad of *soles* and placed it in the woman's uplifted hand. Her mouth dropped open when she saw the money. She looked up at him like he was a saint beamed down from heaven.

After he climbed into the back of the taxi, he glanced up at the huge American flag drooping from the Embassy's flagpole. It was a perfectly breezeless day. Nothing stirring. As he watched the flag dangle limply from its mast, he thought of the dead *campesinos*. The limp flag said it all. A perfect symbol of American foreign policy, he thought, as he slammed the rear door of the cab.

One thing was certain. It would not end here. If it took him the rest of his life, he'd discover what happened to the congressman and how his death was related to Colonel Montero and the Machipa massacre. Senator Kursten had been John Brinton's friend, and Brinton wouldn't sleep lightly tonight, not after what he'd heard today. He'd have John Brinton's cooperation. And if he didn't have it, eventually the story would go to the press. But given the sad state of his reputation as a journalist, he'd need to wait and obtain all the information he could before going public.

ABOUT THE AUTHOR

Most of his adult life, Michael Segedy has lived outside of the United States (Peru, Morocco, Israel, and Taiwan).

Apart from fiction, Michael has published numerous academic articles about literature and writing.

In 1985, Gwendolyn Brooks, poet laureate of Illinois, presented him with *Virginia English Bulletin's* first-place writing award.

Michael and his family currently live in Charlotte, North Carolina and Lima, Peru

Made in the USA
Monee, IL
12 July 2022

43c9a69e-e3b0-4e61-ba7a-8822ac344034R01